Praise for Gayl Jones

'A literary giant, and one of my favourite writers' **Tayari Jones, author of** *An American Marriage*

'Jones's writing powerfully blends narrative and lyricism ... Her imagination seems to thrive on outstripping one's expectations' **Margo Jefferson, author of** *Constructing a Nervous System*

'Gayl Jones is a literary legend ... A once-in-a-lifetime work of literature, the kind that changes your understanding of the world' **Yara Rodrigues Fowler, author of** *there are more things***, on** *Palmares*

'A fascinating meditation on Black female creativity ... Vivid characters shimmer through the pages' *Guardian* **on** *The Birdcatcher*

'As a Black women writer, her truth-telling, filled with beauty, tragedy, humour and incisiveness, is unmatched' **Imani Perry, author of** *Looking for Lorraine*

'Tremendous. A masterfully absorbing, mythic work from a vital voice. The gods have conspired to gift us a new book from Gayl Jones and my what a gloriously eddying read' **Irenosen Okojie, author of** *Nudibranch***, on** *Palmares*

'Page after breathtaking page, her prose is intricate, mesmerizing, and endlessly inventive and subversive' **Deesha Philyaw, author of** *The Secret Lives of Church Ladies***, on** *Palmares*

About the Author

Gayl Jones was born in Kentucky in 1949. She attended
Connecticut College and Brown University, and has taught at
Wellesley and the University of Michigan. Her books include
Corregidora, *Eva's Man*, and *The Healing*, which was a National
Book Award finalist; *Palmares*, which was a finalist for the 2022
Pulitzer Prize in fiction and longlisted for the Rathbones Folio
Prize; and *The Birdcatcher*, which was a 2022 National Book
Award finalist.

THE
UNICORN
WOMAN

GAYL JONES

virago

VIRAGO

First published in the United Stated in 2024 by Beacon Press
First published in Great Britain in 2024 by Virago Press

1 3 5 7 9 10 8 6 4 2

HB ISBN 978-0-349-01691-7
Trade Paperback 978-0-349-01692-4

Text design and composition by Kim Arney
Printed and bound in Great Britain by Clays Ltd, Elcograf S.p.A

Papers used by Virago are from well-managed forests and other responsible sources.

Virago
An imprint of
Little, Brown Book Group
Carmelite House
50 Victoria Embankment
London EC4Y 0DZ

An Hachette UK Company
www.hachette.co.uk

www.virago.co.uk

For my father, Franklin Jones,
a World War II veteran (Army)

And my brother, Franklin Taylor Jones,
a Vietnam veteran (Army and Navy)

But for God's sake, learn to look beneath the surface.

—RALPH ELLISON, *Invisible Man*

By going from spot to spot, talking to this person and that one, I had gotten this reality as it seeped into me from the personalities of others.

—RICHARD WRIGHT, *Black Power*

Are you sure this legend is the real one?

—CHARLES BAUDELAIRE, "Windows"

Come, Sancho, and behold what you have to see but not to believe; make haste, my son, and learn what wizards and enchanters are able to accomplish . . . there are many kinds of enchantment and perhaps they change with the times from one kind to another.

—MIGUEL DE CERVANTES, *Don Quixote*

I figure the unicorn must be good for something.

—ANONYMOUS UNICORN HUNTER

Je suis né avec la dernière disposition à la tendresse, et, comme tous mes efforts n'ont pu vaincre les penchants que j'avais à l'amour, j'ai cherché à me rendre heureux, c'est-à-dire autant qu'on peut l'être avec un coeur sensible. . . .

Vous me direz sans doute qu'il faut être poète pour aimer de cette manière: mais, pour moi, je crois qu'il n'y a qu'une sorte d'amour, et que les gens qui n'ont point senti de semblables délicatesses n'ont jamais véritablement aimé.

—*LES INTRIGUES DE MOLIÈRE*

Why not a black unicorn?

—DUDLEY RANDALL

Everything begins with an idea . . .

—DON STEELE, *Symbolism and Modernity*

CONTENTS

THE
UNICORN
WOMAN

BOOK I

A Young Man's Fancy

I T WAS AT A SPRING CARNIVAL in Central Kentucky, sometime after
the Second World War, that I first saw her. Alone, but nevertheless in a
holiday-making mood, I was strolling about eating a burger and drinking
a Coke when suddenly I spotted a large billboard advertising "The Unicorn
Woman."

Like most of you, I had seen crocodile women, bearded ladies, and
assorted other freaks or, I should say oddities, but I'd never seen a unicorn
woman, genuine or not. Thus, I was curious, especially since there was no
photograph or drawing on the billboard to give a clue, not even the most
ambiguous one, nor did the name Unicorn Woman provide an easy give-
away, like say, for instance, the Bearded Lady: stick a beard on any woman
you see, and that's what you have. Usually it was quite obviously fake.

Standing in front of the tent, I finished the burger, drank the Coke,
and watched other men enter. Some entered straightaway, others waited
nonchalantly at the edges of the crowd, still others glanced about furtively
as if it mattered who saw them go in: Their preachers? Their wives? Their
sweethearts? *Any* stranger? One man even looked thoughtful, as if he were
meditating—contending only with himself about whether or not to enter.
Most of the men wore ordinary workers' or farmers' clothes, but there was
an occasional fancy young man or dandy. There were even a few obviously
wealthy men who entered. After a while, I paid my dime and started to
trot inside.

"Your change, buddy. It's just a nickel."

"Thanks."

"You'll be glad you went in. She's lovely."

I put the change in my pants pocket and entered.

Of course, I had expected to find either a woman in a cage or a unicorn
in one, even though I'd read somewhere that the unicorn was a mythical
beast, which had only existed in the collective imagination. A fabled creature.

A creature of fables, of legend. It appeared only in art and literature, some ancient myth that had origins in India or China. And then had inspired the imaginations of people everywhere. The subject matter of historians and philosophers, and there were even said to be even medicinal cures and medicinal magic in the horn. I tried to remember what the unicorn was a symbol of. Of hope? Of peace? Of freedom? Of spirituality? But there were no such things as unicorns. And to hunt them would be foolish.

The Turks and Greeks and Hebrews had unicorns. Then I wondered if Africans had ever accepted the unicorn myth? Or Indians of America?

Hadn't I read somewhere that the Africans had a name for the unicorn? Okapi? And did not some Indians in America also have the unicorn as a spirit animal in their myths and legends? I tried to remember what I'd read. I tried to remember the origins of the unicorn.

I immediately saw just the back of the woman, who sat on a stool in the middle of a roped-in circle. Viewed from the rear, she looked like any ordinary woman. She was clad in a brown, broad-shouldered, sequined dress, and she was brown herself, which surprised me, as I was used to entering carnival tents only to discover white freaks. Her slender, dimpled arms were the color of my own.

I joined the circle of men and one woman. For some reason, women freaks attracted men more than they did other women. Men freaks, on the other hand, attracted whole families. Even little children. I don't know if this was always the case, or whether one can make a fast rule of it, but whenever I paid my dime or nickel, it was generally the case. And in those days I was a carnival-goer. I enjoyed carnivals, circuses, and state fairs. I liked the food and I liked the spectacle and the amusements.

When I got to the side of her and was able to observe her in profile, I saw the spiraled horn protruding from her forehead like a bull's horn or a goat's: diagonally pointed upward, it was white and shining. Red, black, and white, weren't those supposed to be the colors of a unicorn's horn?

Red at the tip, black in the center, and white at the base? But this horn was one color. White. A white horn protruding from her brown forehead.

I walked around until I finally stood straight in front of her, face-to-face with her. Like a lot of freaks, and a number of theatrical performers, she looked but didn't see you individually. There are tales of performers and entertainers who distinguish people, who behave as if you're the only person in the world when you meet and greet them. But I've found that to not always be true. Well, I saw her. And for that moment, it was like she was the only woman in the world. A real beauty. And the funny thing about it, the horn didn't disturb her beauty; it enhanced it.

I remained in front of her longer than I should have, because the other gents and one lady suddenly shouted, "Get a move on, bud."

I completed my second circle, then my third; I don't know how many turns I took around the woman. I felt indefatigable. Each time I paused before her, I was shouted at to let the others get their chance.

"Get a move on, bud."

"Do you think it's real?" asked the woman.

"It looks real," observed a man. "I bet her forehead's tender, though."

"A lot looks real that ain't," said the woman.

I must admit that the horn did look real. It appeared to be actually growing out of the woman's forehead. Roped-off, she was nevertheless close enough for you to touch, but you didn't dare touch her or her horn. It was sort of an invisible or unspoken rule: you looked but didn't touch, like in a museum with a work of art, even a natural history museum with their exhibits, though there was no sign forbidding it. I wondered whether she'd polished the horn. I imagined her brushing it after she'd brushed her teeth. Some special horn powder or paste. Part of her regular daily make-up routine. And she had the classic style of the age. Well-manicured eyebrows and Vaseline to give a special shine to her red lips. And she was well-groomed.

The horn looked real, like I said, but in those days I did not believe it was.

"I didn't know what I expected to see," said the woman. "I thought it was going to be part unicorn and part woman, not all woman and just that horn sticking out of her forehead."

"Well, I never would've believed anything else," said the man, with a look of appreciation. "I can believe the horn. Plus, the horn's what lets you know she's a unicorn. Wouldn't be a unicorn without a horn."

"Could be a goat," said the woman. "Ain't a unicorn supposed to have a goat's beard anyway? A goat's beard and a lion's tail, not just a horn. I saw a picture of one in an encyclopedia."

"She kinda reminds me of Billie Holiday. Lady Day."

"Every good-looking woman reminds you of Billie Holiday."

Every time I got in front of her, I stayed too long. "Get a move on, bud!" they shouted, yet again.

"That stool should be electrified and *she* should turn," said the woman. "We shouldn't have to turn. She should turn and let us just stand and watch. Look at her. She's an odd creature. She should give me some makeup tips."

The next time I saw her she had an electrified stool that turned, and her audience just stood and watched. Mirrors could have done the trick.

But with mirrors you'd possibly never get to observe the real woman. *"Stop hogging the front; I don't want just the reflection."*

"Move it, Joe."

As I moved, I noticed that whenever there were other displays of cupidity, the people in line waited patiently, talked among themselves till their turn came around; it was only when I hogged the front that the shouts came to get a move on.

I was traveling in Memphis when I saw billboards announcing a traveling carnival in town. I had not stopped thinking of that Unicorn Woman. Whenever I saw a notice of anybody's carnival, especially on days when colored people were free to enter, and allowed to enter, I'd go to see if perhaps the Unicorn Woman was there. Whenever I met a new woman, I couldn't help measuring her against the unicorn one. I didn't always do this consciously, but that underlying feeling persisted: *"She's not the Unicorn Woman."* I suppose most men have some woman that they idealize and measure all others by. Or perhaps most men haven't met their unicorn woman yet, not even in their imaginations and fantasies. But I've met mine, and all I seem to be able to do whenever I encounter any other woman is to shrug. It's not always a visible shrug, though; it's one of those interior shrugs of the spirit. You know the kind.

For instance, one night in Memphis I was out with a woman. Well, a fine thing!, any man would have said of her. Nice, pretty, all of it. It was foggy out, and she wanted to walk in the fog. I don't know why. Some women just have these things they've got to do. Tics, I call them, or fancies, because they're too minor to be obsessions. Maybe she associated the fog with romance. I held onto her elbow and we walked along. I was uncertain of Memphis at the time. I didn't really know the territory, and she was escorting me around the colored sections of the city.

She had introduced me to Parkway Village and Orange Mound. She had introduced me to Lamar Avenue and Getwell Road. She showed me the schools she had gone to: Dunbar Elementary and Melrose High School. She showed me the churches and black-owned businesses in the area.

"Don't you just love the fog?" she asked, as we walked along one of the avenues.

"I've never really thought about it. As something to love, I mean."

Fog had always seemed to me just something to try to avoid getting lost in.

"It's just nice. I don't know what it does to me."

"If you don't know, I certainly don't."

She snuggled up to me. The fog must have made her feel like Marlene Dietrich or Garbo or one of those. In fact, I remember seeing a movie with Garbo on a ship in the fog and she was explaining how the fog did something to her, too, but I've forgotten exactly what it was she said it did, though I believe she said it made her feel holy.

"It makes me feel *new*," she said. "I don't know, it just makes me feel *new*, or something."

I wondered whether "new" had anything to do with romance, or holiness. Maybe either one of them could be her "something." We stood for a moment and peeked in a shoe-store window, then we continued walking.

"This your first time in Memphis?"

"No, I came once with my father when I was a boy. I think we visited Orange Mound, but I'm not sure. He was explaining to me the history of the place, about its being built by and for blacks. I was a little boy, though."

"That's nice. I mean it's always nice to come back to a place where you've been when you were little. Even if you don't exactly remember. That just does something to me."

"Does everything do something to you?"

"No, not everything. But I always just love to go to Miami because the first time I was in Miami I was a little girl. It just does something to me every time I'm there. We had to travel through some places to get there though.

We were in some places where people treated us like we weren't even visible. You'd say something to them and they wouldn't even acknowledge you. And other places where we were too visible. . . . I remember this one little town that had a sign that read 'N_____ read and run, and if you can't read, run anyhow.' They didn't allow colored people in that little town, and we didn't stop where we weren't welcome. My father kept driving. . . . But I adored Miami. And we met this group of Seminole Indians from South Florida who had stayed in Florida, and we met some people from Havana. I didn't know who I was meeting until years later because I was just a small child. All the beaches were white people's–only beaches, then someone directed us to this private beach and then we returned to Miami after the war for the opening of this colored people's beach. All colored people parading up and down the beach. . . . That was lovely. . . . They said some colored people had had a wade-in at one of the white beaches and got themselves arrested. Then they established their own beach. . . . I adore Miami."

"Miami in the fog must be nice," I suggested.

"Oh, but it is! Though I don't exactly remember Miami having fog while I've been there, but it must. Every place has fog. Though every time I've been there, the air's just been as clear as anything. You were a soldier, weren't you?"

"Yeah."

"I can always tell a former soldier." She pronounced it like "farmer soldier." "The way you walk or something. The way you conduct yourself. I guess it's the military training. Maybe it's that or maybe it's the way a soldier looks at a woman. Perhaps not all soldiers . . ."

I looked at her; she giggled.

"A lot of men don't know how to look at a woman, you know. They really don't." She shrugged. "A lot don't even look at you. It's a certain type of acknowledgment, I suppose. And you're always tipping your hat to me. It's a certain type of acknowledgment."

I looked at the fog, at the languid shimmer of the buildings seen through fog. They looked like cardboard buildings, like we were living in some future century where they built only throwaway buildings. Two ghosts came walking toward us: the man ghost tipped his hat, the woman smiled. Then we were able to distinguish them as real. They entered one of the buildings. Music could be heard from within. A songstress singing a song of love.

"I bet he's a farmer soldier," she said.

The woman had looked like one of those adoring types, I thought, but didn't say.

"Did you see a lot of action? I guess that's a silly question, isn't it? All soldiers I've ever met tell me they saw a lot of action. I guess you couldn't be over there overseas during a war and not see a lot of action?"

"With a frying pan."

"What?"

"I was a cook in the army."

"Were you one of those Consciousness Objectors?"

"No."

"So you got to shoot a few too?"

"Yeah, when I was shot at, I got to shoot a few. We were allowed to defend ourselves."

She looked at me, musing, like she was trying to figure out the relative merits of the gun, even in a defensive posture, versus the frying pan, and waiting for me to give my opinion on the subject.

"So you did see *some* action," she said finally, scratching her eyebrows.

"Yeah."

"Yeah," she said, jollily. "I didn't believe you could go over there to a whole war and not see some action, not unless you were a Consciousness Objector—I've met some of those—or one of those colored flyers."

At first I thought she said "colored flours"; then it registered. She was talking about flyers, like the Tuskegee Airmen. But I wondered what was the difference between a whole war and a half war. Maybe we were in the latter all the time. What they called "fighting on two fronts." What they called "double victory." I'd met some men during the war who talked like that.

"I met one of our colored flyers and he said that they just kept training them and retraining them because they didn't know what to do with them for ever so long, at the beginning of the war. I forget what field he was stationed in, but I believe it was somewhere out west. I know about the Tuskegee Airmen, but he was talking about the West. And then he said they finally sent them overseas. They still hadn't figured out what to do with them, but they shipped them overseas anyway. He said he didn't get to see as much action as they could have seen if they'd known what to do with them in the beginning of the war, but he knows airplanes inside and out. I asked him whether there were any colored women who flew planes during the war, but he looked at me like that was a foolish question."

We strolled along, breathing fog. I tried to remember that incantatory passage by Charles Dickens about the fog. *Fog everywhere . . . Chance people.* I'd learned that passage once for a school recitation, but I couldn't remember it now. Something too about a Megalosaurus. Fog moving down the hill like one? Maybe we could meet a Megalosaurus made of fog. Something. Fog in the nostrils? Someone told me once about how foggy Milan is. Because of its geography. I don't know what started the conversation. An Italian American was working in the mess hall along with the blacks. He was a dark-skinned Italian American. Like the Japanese Americans, they'd been considered the enemy. A threat to homeland security. He told me about how they were treated. But he'd joined the army anyway. He was teaching me a few of his favorite Italian recipes and then he started talking about Milan, where his ancestors originated before they came to America. Because of her adoration of the fog, Milan would've been her dream city.

"It would've been nice to have been somebody's deer," she was saying. *Deer?* That's what I heard.

"What do you mean?" I asked. I squeezed her shoulder a bit and pulled her a bit closer.

"Somebody's *deer*," she repeated. "You know. 'Dear So-and-So, I have just landed on foreign soil . . .' and all that. Like when soldiers write their gals letters, you know. Some of the gals collect those letters. I met all my soldiers after the war. None of the fellows I knew before the war were old enough to be soldiers."

"Then you weren't old enough to be somebody's *dear*."

"That's right. I was a youngling during the war. But I still wonder what it was like to be a grown woman during the war. A grown woman and in love, and receiving Dear-So-and-So letters from a soldier. I used to see some of those gals getting their letters from soldiers and writing to them. Some of them weren't that much older than me, but they were still grown women. I used to call them ma'am and some of them would laugh at me. Did you have a dear?"

"No."

"You couldn't have been too old when the war started."

"No, I was eighteen."

"And I'll bet you were a fine young man. To go through a whole war too. That's just awful, not to have had a dear to write letters to. And to have received letters from. I'll bet you have a dear now, though, don't you?" she asked, but answered for me. "Of course you do. All the good ones already have their dears. . . . All the fine ones . . . Are you still a cook?"

"No, I repair tractors."

"You do? You know, one farmer soldier was telling me that they had tanks that could be converted into tractors when the war was over. You know, like interchangeable parts or something. They could either be tanks or tractors depending on if there was a war or not. In peacetimes, they were tractors. In wartimes, they were tanks. I bet you could have repaired a tank. . . ."

"Sure. I can repair just about anything."

"I'll bet. You look like that sort of guy. But I bet they didn't know what to do with you either."

"Probably not."

"That's the same with most of our men. And many of them were eager to do whatever was needed for the war effort. And it's been like that with every war, my papa told me. I wasn't too young to remember that. And the ration books on the home front. And the women going off to work in the factories and the defense plants. I remember all that."

I said nothing.

"Do you want to go in here?" I nodded.

"Yeah, this is a really nice place; you'll like it. They've got a jukebox and sometimes they have live music. They've got a woman who sings songs she wrote herself. Anyway, you look like you've had enough fog. You don't look like you appreciate it as much as I do. I have to remember that everybody doesn't like fog, that fog annoys some people. And especially if you were a flyer. You can't like the fog, for sure. It just does something to me, though. . . . Yeah, I bet you could've repaired a tank or two. Well, as many as you'd wanted, I'd imagine. And I bet you could've converted tanks into tractors, or even tractors into tanks. But I'm sure you could have repaired a tank or two. Well, as many as you'd wanted, I'd imagine. I wonder how many tanks got converted into tractors after the war? Who knows, but you could be repairing a tractor that used to be a tank, like the men repairing tanks that used to be tractors, but of course you'd have to know that though, wouldn't you, I mean with your knowledge and information. I mean, what good are interchangeable parts if they can't be recognized and especially by mechanically inclined and knowledgeable men like yourself?"

I held the door for her as she was talking and we went inside. The door was too solid to be made out of cardboard or any other throwaway thing. Inside, we listened to a woman singing:

Love's such a wonderful thing O yes, O yes, Oh yes.
Love's such a wonderful thing O yes, O yes, Oh yes.
Makes you walk when you walk,
And you're walking so light,
Makes you talk, and you talk
And your talking's just right.
Makes you feel good from morning
Till night.
Yes, love's such a wonderful thing. Oh yes.
Love's such a wonderful thing O yes, O yes, Oh yes.
Love's such a wonderful thing O yes, O yes, Oh yes.
Makes you sing with joy,
And you feel so bright,
Makes you love everybody
That comes in sight
Makes you so happy
And everything's all right,
Yes, love's such a wonderful thing.
Makes you sing with joy,
And you feel so bright.
Makes you love everybody
That comes in sight.

Makes you so happy
And everything's all right,
Yes, love's such a wonderful thing.

Then a Mexican man joined her and sang:

Awnn Taliano, you are the only
One I'm dreaming of, Awnn Taliano,
You are my only love,
Awnn Taliano, until my days
All cease to be,
My Dearest Senorita, come to my
Hacienda with me.
You are my love, my only love,
You're in the stars above,
There in the night,
You're like a flitting dove,
Against the light,
Please, be my own, my dear
You'll always be.
Awnn Taliaino, you are the only One for me,
You are my fair one, Senorita,
And you will always be,
Forget your past love affair
And come with me.

And they sang together the following song:

Down that bull, here he comes a-charging,
Down that bull, here he comes a-charging,
Down that bull, here he comes a-charging,
Please oh! matador.
Down that bull, put him in his grave now,
Down that bull, put him in his grave now,

Down that bull, put him in his grave now,
Please oh! matador.
If he kills you I will die.
I could not stand to live.
Down him now, before I cry. Your life I cannot bear to give.
So now you down that bull,
Here he comes a-charging,
Down that bull, here he comes a-charging,
Down that bull, here he comes a-charging.
Please oh! matador.

Though no unicorn woman, the woman sitting across from me is very attractive. Both her hair and her skin are reddish brown. Her hair, swept back from her narrow forehead, is so closely the color of her skin that even with the different texture, it's still almost hard to tell where her forehead ends and her hair begins. This makes her forehead look broad and full except for one thin line of gray streaking catercornered from the center of her hairline. She's got a longish, pointy nose, but it doesn't distract from her face and seems paradoxically to focus your attention more fully on her expressive, slanted eyes, which are brownish black and dart about as if there were things about her worth looking at, or looking for. When they land on my face, they seem a bit surprised or startled. Her eyebrows are zig-zagged from her constantly scratching them as if she's got dandruff of the brows—perhaps another tic, perhaps nerves. Her mouth is somewhat biggish, but she had painted it in such a way that it looks smaller, more full than big. Sometimes she purses it or closes her lips together as if to even out her strawberry lipstick. The mole on the corner of her right jaw jumps out of sight when you look at her full-faced but becomes nicely visible when she turns sideways. In fact, seen in profile, the mole enhances her face, slightly alters its character, so that she doesn't seem merely attractive but almost a beauty. There are barely perceptible lines in her young forehead, but I notice them because they have the same pattern as the lines on my own, shaped like a T with double lines at the top. I wonder what those people who read foreheads would say. Her teeth are small, regular, and white. Indeed, they are so regular and sparkling that they look as if they've been filed then whitewashed. She smiles at me, showing them off. She could be somebody's darling. Anybody's dear. That is, if you didn't know the Unicorn Woman existed.

"So have you moved to Memphis, or is this just a vacation?" she asks.

I thought I'd already answered, but I reply, "Just a vacation."

"I used to think I'd like to move to Miami," she says. "I know it's the Deep South. But it doesn't seem like the South South. It seems to have its own character. I think it's nicer to have a place like that to go to, though. It makes it . . . I don't know what the word is I'm looking for."

"Special," I offer.

"Yeah, special," she repeats. "I like 'special.' That wasn't exactly the word I was looking for, but I like it."

Her blouse, peeking out from the lapels of her dark cotton jacket, is lacy and white and makes you want to touch it, so I do.

"You're very forward, aren't you?" she says, giving me a look of discreet indulgence. "Men like to call some women forward, but a man's more forward than a woman any day."

She takes my hand off her blouse and puts it atop the bowl of salted pretzels. I give her one, and she leans back and crunches.

"Do they call you forward?" I inquire.

She crunches a moment, swallows, sips a little beer, then replies, her look tender, "Yeah, they do. But I'm not half as forward as they think I am." She pauses. "Nor half as backward either." She reflects. "But I think you have to be at least a little forward, don't you? To get by in this world, you have to be a little forward. And at least a little forward-thinking, too, don't you think?"

Her questions are rhetorical, so I don't answer.

"I can tell you're a good guy though, forward or not," she says, raising one of the jagged brows. "And you seem like an intelligent sort. I don't think you haven't got a dear, though. Or at least someone you *wish* you had."

But as I was saying, I was also in Memphis when I saw the Unicorn Woman for the second time. Seeing a sign advertising a traveling carnival in town, I

went and discovered the Unicorn Woman was there. So I paid my dime—
the price had been raised—and entered straightaway. This time she had an
electric stool or, if not electric, some mechanism that made it turn. I just
stood in one place, and she kept turning toward me, her horn pointing up
like an arrow.

"Look at that."

"I wonder if she was born with it or if it just grew sometime afterward.
Mighta been a full grown woman when she growed that horn."

"Well, if she'da had it when she was born, it musta tore somebody."

"Oh, it couldn't've been more than a gristle then. And then as she
grew . . ."

"I just might believe in it."

"I think she musta been a full-grown woman to have growed a horn that
fancy. I don't believe she grew that horn until she grew up."

"I just might believe in it."

"They never let you touch 'em. Look but don't touch. That's the policy.
That's the rule. You have to see to believe."

"Looky there."

"I wish she'd turn slower, so I could get a real good look."

"You certainly have to see to believe."

"I prefer the bearded lady myself. That ain't natural neither, but it's more
natural than that. A beard is more natural than a horn, even if it is on a lady."

"I'm not such a fool to believe everything I see."

"She looks like she's straight out of a fairy tale, don't she?"

"A mythology book, or a fantasy, or what they call that scientific fiction."

"I don't believe it. They don't have colored unicorns. All the unicorns
I've ever seen have been white."

"I don't believe it anyhow, colored or not. But colored seems to make it
more impressive and more unusual. Any unicorn can be white."

"Suppose we all had those horns, though? That would be something,
wouldn't it? If every human being had a horn?"

"Yes, it would sure be something. But if we all had horns, it would just
be a natural thing. We probably wouldn't even notice it, unless the horns
all had different shapes and colors."

"I should have worn my overshoes, all that mud outside, and people traipsing it in here too."

"It looks dangerous, don't it, that horn? I bet you could sharpen it like you would a pencil."

"No, you'd have to file it."

"I wouldn't want her to butt me with that."

"I once saw her in Kansas City and again in Atlanta."

"I'd like to take that broad out, to a fancy dinner or a movie."

"Just be careful. Don't let her butt you with that horn."

"She reminds me of a songstress."

"I wonder what it feels like having that horn."

"Like your teeth, I would imagine. Do you feel your teeth?"

"Sure you do."

"It's made out of the same stuff as fingernails, I bet, or your hair. They say that's the same stuff."

"I wonder what she eats."

"Oats and barley, like a goat or a little lamb. Ha."

"She's a human woman; she ain't no goat or a lamb. I like oats and barley."

"What freak do you want to see next?"

"What they got?"

"They ought to have music in here."

When I got outside, I asked the man what the unicorn woman's name was.

"The Unicorn Woman."

"Does she have a name, like Sally, Sue, Gloria, Evelyn?"

"Ziga something. Dalan, that's right. Ziga Dalan."

"What kind of name is that?"

"That's her name, bud. I don't make 'em."

"Any chance of getting to meet her?"

"Up close and personal?"

"Yeah."

"Not a chance, bud. Our freaks don't fraternize with the general public." He must have liked the alliteration because he repeated it. "Our freaks don't fraternize."

(I remember years later going to a traveling carnival and seeing exactly that sign: OUR FREAKS DON'T FRATERNIZE. I was certain that he'd inspired it. Or that indirectly, *I'd* inspired it, because that was his answer to *my* question.)

Except for the horn, Ziga Dalan, if that was her true name, didn't look freakish to me. I paid the man another dime to go in and see her again.

Standing in a shadowy corner, I waited until she turned toward me. Whether or not her name was authentic, it was good to know it. It added a dimension to her, though whenever I think of her I can't think "Ziga" or even "Dalan"; I must think "Unicorn Woman," perhaps because that was the first name I met her by. And "Unicorn Woman" intrigued me more than any name.

I stayed until the tent closed, then hung around outside until one of the carnival security men said, "Get a move on, bud." I had not seen the Unicorn Woman exit, though I stood at such an angle so I could observe both the front and back of the tent. I was certain she hadn't exited.

Perhaps she'd waited until assured that all strangers and stragglers, like me, were off the grounds before she left, in order to keep the mystery and her privacy.

"Get a move on, bud."

The funny thing is my real name *is* Bud—Buddy Ray Guy. So whenever people think they're calling me *out of my name*, they are actually calling me *by* name.

"You know how to boil water, Bud?" asked Ben Boone, the sergeant in charge of the mess.

"Yes, sir," I said, saluting.

"The last guy they sent back here didn't know how to boil water, didn't know beans from potatoes. You sure you can boil water, Bud?"

"Yes, sir."

"What's your name, Private?"

"Bud, sir."

"I hope you're not another wise guy. I don't like wise guys."

"Sir, it *is* Bud. Private Buddy Ray Guy."

"Another wise guy. I don't like you."

I showed him my tags.

"Private Bud Guy. So it is. I bet your middle name ain't Ray. I bet it's Wise. Bud Wise Guy. Dalton, show this wise guy the ropes."

I can't help it. Whenever anybody says that I start looking for ropes.

Instead, I was handed an apron. Well, it did have strings attached.

For a while in the army, I was nicknamed Budwiser. I couldn't tell whether a fellow was calling for me or a beer.

Granger works on one tractor and I work on another. Sometimes we're hidden from each other between tractors and he's all voice.

Sometimes we work on different sides of the same tractor. Either way, he's all voice.

"Enjoy your vacation?"

"Yeah, sure."

"Where'd you go?"

"Memphis."

"The big M, huh? Well, I guess Miami's the big M, though, ain't it?"

"Probably."

"You headed south. I thought a fellow like you would've headed up north. Memphis must be the little M, unless you're from Milwaukee. I was in Memphis once. Seemed like a nice place to visit."

I laugh.

His head darts up for a moment, then he's concealed by the tractor again.

"I enjoyed it."

"That sounds like a woman to me. Only reason I know for a fellow like you to head south is on account of a woman."

I turn a screw. The hard-packed ground I'm working on is incised with tractor tracks and footprints. It's like standing on some sort of clay mosaic. There's no grass in the space we work, a section of yard framed on one side by the concrete rectangular office building and on the three other sides by a high, wire fence. Stacks of lumber are arranged against the fence on the street side, for whatever purpose I've never guessed. Much of the wood has dry rot. Perhaps this used to be a lumberyard before it was converted into a tractor repair yard.

"You know, when I was younger I used to like to travel during my vacations. And a man like me's best suited for the Southern states. Now, I've been fixing tractors for twenty years, and my idea of a good vacation is . . . Do you know what my idea of a good vacation is?"

"What?"

"To go home and hug on Charlotte; that's my wife."

Chuckle.

"Well, I guess that's traveling of another variety."

"Yeah."

"You ain't married are you, Bud?"

"No way."

"That's because you're still a youngster."

"Not so young."

"Youngster to me. I'm an old man compared to you. And you let the army claim you before a woman did. That always ruins a man for a while. But listen to me talking. I missed two wars. Too young for World War I and too old for World War II. Too young for one war and too old for th' other. I'm from the between-the-wars generation. I don't know what sort of person that makes me or my generation. I don't even know if they have a name for my generation. . . . And then, of course, I let a woman claim me."

Pliers.

"Me and the wife did take a camper and go south to fish. Not the deepest South, because sometimes I'm mistaken there. Still I enjoyed catching her more than I did the fish. I enjoyed catching Charlotte more. That sounds like the name of a book, don't it? *Catching Charlotte*. I like some Mark Twain, speaking of booksters, and by the way her maiden name is Finn. Charlotte Finn. But still I think that says a lot about a man, when he stays passionate even unto old age. Passionate old men can be wondrous. And when he lets a woman claim him before anything else . . . I mean, I'm one of the best tractor fixers around, if I do say so myself, but what does that really say about a man?"

"That you're one of the best tractor fixers around."

"You're darn right. How'd you get to be so smart? But what does that really say about a man?"

Jumble of wires. I unjumble.

"I don't know."

"You're right, you don't know. Even the wisest men don't know. When I was a youngster, I didn't know. Here I am now, and I still don't know. And as a youngster I couldn't imagine myself passionate even unto old age. Maybe a man's defined by love. They say that about a woman, and sometimes define a woman by love, but it might also be true about a man. All I know's I enjoy tractor fixing. It's the second thing I do enjoy. It's still working with your hands, right?"

I flinch. "I think the mind's in there somewhere."

"You better believe it. The mind directs the handy work. And that ain't just whistling Dixie. Pardon me. So who was the woman?"

"Nobody special."

"Had to been somebody special, or you'd spill the beans. You'd be telling stories and tales about her. That you keep her to your private self means she's special."

"Charlotte's special and you spilled the beans."

"I didn't spill 'em, Bud, I just shook 'em a bit. Anyway, Charlotte's my wife. Did you ever hear the difference between a wife and a girlfriend?"

"What?"

"With a wife you can't do nothing right. With a girlfriend you can't do nothing wrong. That's a joke, Bud, and it's not exactly the truth. But you know, Bud, you're right for sticking up for working with your hands and for the intelligence in the matter. And for the intelligence of the working man. Because you know in the old days, in yesteryear, the artist was considered to be very low on the totem pole because he worked with his hands. Then it took somebody like Michangelo or the Renaissance that raised the status of the artist to the level that we think of artistic men today. People probably said, 'Hey, wait a minute, the mind's in there somewhere.' Then the artist climbed the totem pole. But in yesteryear if you were an artist, you worked with your hands, period. You and me, Bud, we're artists of tractor fixing. I suppose tractor fixing is an art."

He works a moment, then he resumes, "I learned that tidbit from Charlotte's cousin who's a schoolteacher. She don't come a-calling unless she teaches you something. That's what she believes in. She will teach anybody anywhere and anytime and not just in the classroom. She doesn't limit herself to the classroom. Anyway, it raised my status just to hear talk like that, about the work of artistic men. Sometimes she will talk about artists, but in the olden times artists generally referred to men. She says that some folks are beginning to study the role of women in art and the history of art and that maybe the original artists were women. She says that we have always been under the assumption that the cave drawings were done by men, but it's possible that not a few of them were done by women.

"Charlotte's cousin says there's a whole history of women artists that hasn't been told yet. If it was up to her, she'd rewrite the whole history of art herself."

I wait for him to chuckle. It's slow this time, but it comes.

"Are you going to drive yours out?" he asks. He means the tractor.

"Yeah."

"Whose farm?"

"Hennebelle."

"Who's gonna pick you up? Ranch?"

"Yeah. Ranch."

"That means that they'll send Cerf for me. Talk your ear off, that fellow does."

I say nothing. He works in silence for a moment, then he says, "You know, when those artists got their status, they started doing the silliest things. A man don't need status if it makes him crazy. Charlotte's cousin told me all the crazy things them artist fellows used to do. She even mentioned a few artist womenfolks, like I said. They didn't seem half so crazy as the fellows, though, and the fellows even had the higher status, and are glorified in the history of art. Well, you learn a lot when there's a schoolteacher in the family. I don't know what to do with most of the stuff she's teaching me, except sometimes to use it in a conversation, like I'm doing now, so to speak. . . . Hennebelle? I shoulda recognized that tractor."

"What do you mean?"

"Because it looks like somebody bombed it. I hear you laughing. I knew you'd appreciate a good joke. . . . Yeah, Ranch is decent, but with Cerf, you can't get a word in edgewise."

There's a professor who works at Kentucky State College in Frankfort, one of the historical black colleges—it was referred to as Kentucky State Industrial College in the earlier days—teaching biology, anatomy, physiology, you know, the premedical sciences. I call to make an appointment with him. As he's on vacation, I leave my name and address with a secretary. Several weeks later I receive a postcard informing me when Professor Blake will be available. I call again, and when an appointment is accorded me, I drive up there one Friday afternoon.

The college is located on a hill. During the flood of '33, people fled to the college for safety, since it was the highest point and a place of refuge. I park at the bottom of the hill and walk up, taking a few bounding leaps to get my nerve up, or my energy. Professor Blake is in his office sitting behind a tiny walnut desk. Behind him on the pale green wall is a multicolored painting showing the human interior. I'm sweating a bit when I enter.

"Professor Blake?" I inquire.

"Come in." He peers at me up over his horn-rimmed glasses. The room smells like peppermint candy mints and armpits, though I can't be sure whether they're his or mine.

"Are you one of my farmer students?" he asks. That's how he pronounces "former," even though he's a professor.

"No, sir."

"I didn't think you were. I always remember my farmer students. You do look kind of familiar though. Take a seat."

I sit in the seat reserved for students and "farmer" students. I stare for a second at the tiny red pineal gland on the anatomy and physiology chart, read the small print that says "function uncertain," then I look at him and explain.

"I have an aunt who went to high school with you, sir, so I sort of know of you through her. She also took refuge here up on the hill at the college during the flood of '33. Perhaps I resemble her." I start to add that I also know him by reputation, since this is, after all, a college and he has an academic reputation, but I seem to be overexplaining and maybe talkative out of nervousness, and decide that knowing him through my aunt is good enough.

"What's your aunt's name?" he inquires.

"Maggie Guy."

"Maggie Guy?" He looks bewildered for a moment, then he smiles. "Yes, I do believe I know Maggie Guy; yes, I do believe I remember her. So you're Maggie's boy?"

"I'm her nephew, sir."

"Nephew, yes." He keeps nodding. "Yes, she does ring a bell. Yes, I do believe we did go to high school together. I think I do remember a little Maggie even from kindergarten. I think we went all through the school years together, until I went off to college. Yes, indeed."

I say nothing.

"Margaret Guy. Her true name is Margaret, isn't it?"

"Yes, sir."

"Of course I know Margaret. Mag, we also used to call her. So you're Mag's boy?"

"Nephew."

"Yes, of course. Well, I actually certainly do remember Margaret Guy, if I remember correctly. And perhaps you do resemble her. That's probably why I thought I knew you. So you're interested in enrolling in one of my courses, are you? Want to become a doctor, do you, young man?"

"No, sir."

"You don't? Then why are you enrolling in my courses? They're all premed courses. I like to keep them reserved for our future doctors. We need to set that priority. I keep them open for our future doctors first and foremost, and then I allow the otherwise interested."

"No, sir; let me explain. That's not what I mean. I mean, I don't wish to enroll in any of your courses. I don't wish to become a doctor. I'm here because I want to ask you a question about human anatomy."

"You're a little too old for that, aren't you, boy?" he chuckles.

"I didn't mean to express it like that, exactly."

"What's on your mind, young man? I'm certainly available to answer your questions. That's why this college was established. For the Mental Improvement of the Negro. And I'm its humble servitor."

I flinch and think of how as a boy I'd tried to get some of the kids in the neighborhood to join a club that I'd pompously called "The Society for the Mental Improvement of the Negro." I thought that we'd read books and exchange books and discuss and explore the ideas in them. I suppose

it would be a sort of book club. I thought the other kids would be excited
by the idea, but they had merely laughed at me and ridiculed me for my
pomposity. I'd felt resentful that the other kids had not been as interested in
moral and mental improvement as I had been. Now when I heard my words
echoed back to me by the professor, I understood the joke. Why did it sound
so funny? But Professor Blake wasn't joking. He waited for my question.

"Yes?" He prods my silence. "Don't be skittish, young man. I teach
future doctors, after all. And I've heard many questions. Even small, foolish
questions."

Hoping mine is not a small, foolish question, I proceed to tell him about
the Unicorn Woman. I ask him whether it's indeed possible anatomically
and physiologically for a real human woman to have a horn growing out
of the center of her forehead, as if she were a goat or a ram.

He looks at me. At first I think it's because I'd indeed asked a small and
foolish question, then dismissing that, I think his look is because I'd said
"human woman," which was redundant. If someone's a woman, they are
indeed human. But he looks at me again and seems confused.

Then he gives me another look. Wary?

He peers around at the chart of the human interior. He looks back at
me, this time bellicose.

"What's your name, boy?"

"Buddy Ray Guy."

"Well, Mr. Guy," he recites, "in the annals of time and human history
and the world, man has discovered many things about the human being,
many manifestations and phenomena that many consider impossible or
improbable. Therefore, it's not totally inconceivable for a human woman
to have such a manifest phenomenon. There are marvels to behold." Then
he whispers, leaning forward, "Does that answer your question?"

"Uh, yes, uh, yes, sir," I stutter.

"But I will say, Mr. Guy, that I've visited many natural history museums,
and I've seen the horns of many animals from modern day to prehistoric
times, but I've yet to see the horn of a human being, except maybe a cornet."

He guffaws, blowing out air and spittle, then he leans back in his chair,
his hands perched on his small stomach; he waits. I chuckle a bit and nod.
He gives another horse laugh, looks gratified, and then he speaks.

"You're Maggie Guy's boy all right, you certainly are. Maggie ought to know better than to send you here to try to kid me. You can't kid a kidder. He'll just kid you right back every time. Tell her I threw your joke right back at you, and that I was ready, you hear? I've known Maggie since we were in preschool. She's an old-time kidder herself. She used to be the class jokester. She was both serious and a clown. We were the two smartest kids in our class, and in a bit of a competition with each other.

"Well, you tell Maggie howdy for me. Send you around here to try to kid me. I'm Professor J. Kidder, that's who I am. Yessiree. Don't ask me what that J. stands for or I'll kid you again. Well, you tell Maggie howdy for me. You tell her I've got a few jokes and riddles still left up my own sleeves."

"Yes, sir."

"Tell her I enjoyed that one. A woman with a horn. That joke was inspired and refreshing. There's no drought like a joker's drought. I'm around serious-minded people all the time, and we've got a lot to be serious about, but I appreciate a good joke every now and then. You're Mag's boy all right. Nice to meet you, my boy. Tell Mag I enjoyed your joke, and you tell her mine, you hear?, about the cornet, tell her I throwed the joke right back at you, and that I was ready, you hear? I never was ready for her jokes when I was a boy, but I'm ready now. Tell Maggie to come by and see me herself sometimes. We were kids together, like I said. You send Mag around here, you hear?"

My aunt Maggie Guy is a doily maker. You know what doilies are.

Little lace-like things that come in all shapes and sizes, usually white, but they can be any color. You crochet them. Aunt Maggie has doilies everywhere—on the arms and backs of sofas and chairs, on tabletops, atop the mantelpiece, atop the radio. Anywhere you look where there's an empty space, she fills it with a doily. There are even doilies hanging from the walls as if they were works of art, and perhaps hers should be.

Anybody who needs a doily knows where to go. She does her biggest business around Christmastime, when she especially sells what she calls "The Giant Doily," which can be hung on the wall like a tapestry or one of those religious handkerchiefs. I've forgotten their names, but you've seen them, imprinted with holy images or pilgrims. Once a white man even came to her house because he had heard from his housekeeper, Romain Pavan, one of Aunt Maggie's neighbors, about her giant doilies and wanted to see them for himself.

"You ought to advertise in the newspapers," he told her. "I can help you promote the giant doily and make it famous."

When Aunt Maggie didn't say a word to him or show any sign of excitement or enthusiasm, he said as he held one of the giant doilies aloft and waved it in the air, "Well, why don't you let me draw you up an advertisement and show you what we'll do for you. I'm an advertising man. Then if you'll agree, I'll have you sign our standard contract. If I were a huckster, I'd have you sign the contract first. But I'm an honest man. And you will have your picture in the paper. Well, how about that, Miss Guy?

"Plus, as an additional enticement, I will mock-up a sample ad for you and bring it around for you to look at and ruminate on." And then he pulled out a sketch pad and did a quick mock-up for her.

"No, thank you, sir."

I don't know why my aunt decided not to let the man help her promote her doilies to a larger audience and make them and her famous.

Something in the ad mock-up must have offended her. He was going to promote the doilies as AUNT MAGGIE'S ORIGINAL GIANT DOILY, then there was a drawing of the giant doily, and beside that a space for Aunt Maggie's picture. In the smallest print he had written "caveat emptor," which Aunt Maggie took to be his name. In italics underneath the drawing of the doily he had written "Handmade by Aunt Maggie herself." I suppose Aunt Maggie simply preferred to be a private person, my aunt, but not everybody's aunt. But, like I said, she's got doilies everywhere, every empty space, and she does her best business at Christmas and Eastertime. And there's even a doily that resembles the American flag.

Aunt Maggie is the next person I tell about the unicorn woman and I wait for her reaction.

"Did you say anything to this woman?" she asked.

"Nobody said anything to her. People just talked about her and around her."

"You could've said something to her, seems like to me." She held up a doily to see how it looked in the light.

"It's just something that's not done, sort of an invisible law," I explained. "You just look at those kinds of people, oddities, you don't talk to them."

"Well, I said something to a bearded lady once, an oddity or not. I was just seven though. If I were a grown woman, maybe I wouldn't have said a thing, considered her too strange, but I was a little girl. I talked to her like you'd talk to any natural woman, and she talked right back. I asked her if her beard itched, and she said yes it did. Maybe the next time you should say something to her, invisible law or not. Oddity or not. Treat her like a natural woman. I know you're not a boy, you're a grown man. But speak to her."

"Maybe."

"Okay, *Maybe*." ("Maybe" is who she called me, whenever I answered her that way.)

She held her doily like a half mask and stared at me across it, then she put it on the table. We were sitting at her dining room table, full of doily tools and doily fabric. Everybody called it her "doily table" instead of her dining room table. It was a huge walnut table and seemed the finest, most expensive piece of furniture she possessed. She never served food on it, though, but kept it exclusively for doily making and would take her dinner guests into the living room or the kitchen. She did not like to rearrange her doily stuff just to have a place to eat fancy, as she expressed it. Here, though, she had poured me a small glass of some cherry liqueur, which I was sipping. She must have sipped it often, because her breath always smelled like cherries.

"What else you got to say about her?" she asked, on account of my silence.

"I went to see that professor you went to school with."

"I never went to school with no professor."

"Professor Blake at KSC."

"Harry wasn't no professor when I went to school with him. Just this shiny little boy who knew how to say his alphabet backwards. Did he tell you we were the two smartest kids at our school? What'd you go see him about?"

"To ask him if he thought the horn was real."

She laughed a moment, then she asked, "What'd he tell you?"

"He thought it was a joke. He thought that you'd put me up to it. To kid him. He said you two were smart, but you were a couple of jokesters."

Crocheting what looked like a difficult stitch, she said nothing for a moment, then, "Remembered me, did he? Did he remember me right off, or did you have to nudge him?"

"I had to nudge him."

"Hmm. Well, what you ought to do is to go see one of those herb doctors, root doctors some people call them. Herbalists. They see all sorts of strange sights, people who wouldn't go to an ordinary doctor or doctor's doctor, or would be too embarrassed. Though I suppose that ordinary doctors have seen some curiosities. But a root doctor ought to be able to tell you whether your sight is real or not. They have seen strange and amazing things. I know this woman in Midway who's a herbalist. She's not a doctor's doctor like Harry Blake. I'll write her name and address for you."

She got up, hunting for paper and pencil, and finally came back with a torn piece of brown paper bag and a stubble of a yellow pencil. She scribbled, then handed the paper to me.

"You would not know she's a jigaboo by looking at her, either," she said. "She looks like an Irish woman."

I put the paper in my shirt pocket and sat and watched her make another intricate crochet stitch. I stared at the straws in her small, pierced ears. She kept straws in them when she wasn't wearing earrings, to keep the holes from closing. I sipped the cherry liqueur.

"But you men tickle me," she said suddenly. Twisting her threads she looked like a weaverbird, or Eliot's beneficent spider. In fact, she studied birds' nests and spiderwebs, she said, because they gave her new ideas and enhanced ideas she already had about creating doilies. Likewise, she said, did the veins of leaves and the way that roots grew.

"What?" I asked.

"I don't know. Y'all just do. All of you men. You got all this concern in the world about whether or not the woman's horn is real. And supposing what if it ain't real? Supposing what if it's a fake horn? Does that make her a fake woman? You men just tickle me silly. If I went to a carnival show and saw a horned man, a unicorn man, that I liked and that took my fancy, I wouldn't worry me a bit about whether the horn was real or not. I would spend my time wondering about what the natural man was like."

"I do wonder what the woman's like," I defended. "It's just . . . maybe it's easier to ask people about the horn than the woman. I can't really ask anyone about the woman. The reality of the horn. . ."

"Maybe you've got something there," she interrupted, twisting a thread and knotting it. "Maybe you have. I still don't believe a fake horn makes a fake woman though. I believe she's as natural as any other woman. And I don't doubt she's as beautiful as you say she is. But you got to decide what interests you most—the horn or the woman. 'Will you still love me without my wig?'"

"Aunt Maggie, what're you talking about?"

"This man Catherine Hanuman married. She asked him—man named Sugar McGee—some people called him Cup o'Sugar. She asked him, 'Will you still love me without my wig?' He said he would and they got married. Well, he is somewhere in Kansas City today, I believe. Listen to you laughing. You think it's not like that, don't you? Well, I have known people brighter and more sophisticated than Kate and Sugar, plus sober when they got married, but their reactions are still the same. A wig can be anything. A horn can be a wig. A horn can be anything. Will you still love her without her horn?"

"She still seems the most interesting woman in the world to me." I shrugged. "And I'll admit, I haven't seen anyone more beautiful."

"I believe that's what Sugar said about Kate Hanuman."

I laughed again.

"I hope she doesn't take too much pride in her horn. . . . So you said you had to nudge Harry to remember me?"

"Yes, ma'am."

"Was it a heavy nudge or a light one?"

"Light."

"And you know something? I bet it wasn't even *me* he remembered. I bet he just remembered my *horn*." She smiled. "I ain't gonna tell you what my horn *is* though. But I bet it wasn't *me* he remembered at all."

"He said you oughta come by and see him yourself sometimes."

"Hare said that?" She mused. "Uh, uhm." She smiled again. "Maybe that's all I want him to remember is my horn, anyway. And how smart I used to be as a girl." She gave a laugh that you could barely hear. "Maybe that's all I do want him to remember. Well, anyway, you ought to go over to Midway to see that woman, that herbalist doctor. She looks like an Irish woman, so don't be mistaken. Maybe she can tell you something you want to know about that Unicorn Woman. If not, I think you ought to try talking to that horned woman herself, if you see her again. I believe any woman likes to be talked to, horned or not. Of course, I might be wrong.

"My understanding of other womenfolk might be wrong. Sometimes I don't even understand my own self. You never know what's possible with people, though, do you?" She looked like she was pouting. "Maybe one of these days if I get really curious enough, I might go up there to that college and see exactly what it is that Harry Blake does remember. I know he teaches doctors how to be doctors, that's why I call him a doctor's doctor.

"That was always his dream and wish, to be a medical man."

"She's very cultured," says Grange, while repairing a tractor. "She can tell you who people are that I've never heard of. Blanche—that's the schoolteacher's name and my wife's cousin—well, she says she believes that culture is a myth, but she feels obliged to take it with her wherever she goes. I can't buy that. That's one thing that Blanche says that I can't buy. How can culture be a myth? Culture is culture. It's not mythology. But I've got to give it to Blanche. She knows hordes of people from historical times to the present day that I've never heard of, and I learn somebody new every time she comes to visit. It was Botticelli yesterday. Brueghel came last Sunday. Aristotle, Saint Thomas Aquinas, Boccaccio, Vico, Kant have been there. She brought Confucius with her once, but I already knew him. When I was in school, Confucius used to say as much as Simon."

She looks like any ordinary country woman sitting on her front porch in a wicker chair, catching breeze, barefoot and wearing a colorful starched apron—copper, green, orange. Because she's fair-skinned I momentarily mistake her for a white country woman. In fact, after the war, I saw women all over little villages in Southern France who looked exactly like her. And there's a touch of the Irish, as my aunt said. A bunch of concord grapes are in her lap. Their rich odor drifts toward me. A chicken squawks, rises,

then settles, and chases a duck. In the yard there are lots of chickens and
ducks running about or pecking corn. One bantam rooster perches on the
low branch of a walnut tree whose leaves, sunlight behind them, look like
they're made out of metal. The fence in front is entwined with honeysuckle
vines; you can't tell whether the fence is wire or wood. In the back of the
house, there's an orchard—apple trees, cherry trees, and more walnut trees.
A grape arbor encircles the whole. There are wildflowers. Milkweed and
morning glories. Goldenrod, bloodroot, Virginia bluebells. And there are
the kinds of flowers that attract birds and butterflies. She also has aloe plants
and other healing and medicinal-looking plants. There's a generous cabbage
and lettuce patch to attract the likes of Peter Rabbit or is that Brer Rabbit?

I stand for a moment appreciating the fresh air and the green countryside. Casual, watching me, the woman seems waiting for me to speak.

"Are you Miss Vinnie Leeds?" I ask, finally.

She looks a bit surprised at first, as if she doesn't recognize her own
name, then she says, "Yes, I'm Vinnie Leeds. Come up on the porch, sir."

I climb steps to the yard, head up the concrete walk, then climb more
steps to the porch.

She peers at me. "Sit down and I'll be with you in a minute, sir," she
says, indicating the other wicker chair as she spits grape seeds into her palm,
then tosses them into the yard. The chickens and ducks come running for
them. She offers me some grapes. I shake my head as she explains, "I want
to finish listening to *Amos 'n' Andy* on the radio. Most people know not to
come when it's *Amos 'n' Andy* time, but you are new to me. I've never seen
you before. Whoever told you about me should have told you about my
radio shows. Everybody that knows me knows that I have special radio shows
that I listen to, and *Amos 'n' Andy* is one of them. I keep to my schedule."

I don't remember what Amos and Andy were saying, but I'll make up
something:

> *How'd you like the races, Andy?*
> *I liked them fair enough, Amos. I won.*
> *Well, you are not looking like a man when he wins.*
> *Well, I won at the races, but I lost to Kingfish.*
> *How in the world did you lose to Kingfish?*

Well, when I got back, I told Kingfish that I had won and he says, 'I bet you
    don't know how much you won,' and I said, 'I bet you don't.'
And you meant to say, 'I bet I do too.'
Andy, he had reformulated the construction of the interrogation, leaving out
    the I, and took you off-guard.
Yeah, he tricked me.
Andy, you trick yourself when you don't listen. That was really a numbskull
    thing to do. You knew how much you had won.
Well, I'm not going back to the races.
Why aren't you going back to the races?
I don't want to lose to Kingfish again.
Good night, Andy.
Good night, Amos.
(in unison) Good night, folks in radio land.

She turns off the radio. "That Andy is something else, ain't he? Seems like it needed another line in there, don't it? I think that Amos should have told Andy he shouldn't go back to Kingfish, not to the races." She laughs. I think she tells me her other favorite show is *Perry Mason*, when it was a radio show, before the days of television. And there are some romantic radio shows she likes to listen to, but I don't remember their names.

"What can I do for you, sir?" she asks. "I certainly don't recall ever having seen you."

"My name is Buddy Ray Guy. I was recommended to you by Maggie Guy, my aunt. I mean, you were recommended to me by her."

"Well, come into my parlor," she says, rising.

I'm expecting her parlor to be untidy, but when I get in there it's spick-and-span. I don't see any herbs and potions cluttering up the place. It's sparsely furnished with a sofa, a large soft armchair, a walnut coffee table, and a small bookcase made of cherry-tree wood. This later is likewise sparse, containing only a Bible, a volume of Shakespearean plays, Ovid's *Metamorphosis*, John Bunyan's *The Pilgrim's Progress*, Claude McKay's *Banjo*, Dante's *The Divine Comedy*, Cervantes's *Don Quixote*, and Lewis Carroll's *Through the Looking-Glass*. There's also a book on human physiology, another on plant biology, a dictionary, James Joyce's *Dubliners*, a collection of American humor, and a book on Greek mythology. There are several coffee-table books: *How Does Your Garden Grow?*, *Conchology: A Beginner's Introduction*, and a travel book called *Baffin Island*, which I'd first misread as *Baffling Island*. There are a couple of books on the Hawaiian Islands and Hawaiian history and some books about Native Americans and Africans. Another reads *Irish Fairy Stories, Folktales, Legends and Myths*. There are several pamphlets, the kind that appear to be self-publications. One of the pamphlets is entitled *A Guide to the Medicinal Plants of Kentucky: Barks, Leaves, Stems, Roots, Flowers, Seeds* . . . Underneath the title, written in Latin, is "Periculosum est modicum sapere."

She sees me glance at the brochure and says, "Yes, sir, a little knowledge is a dangerous thing."

It's a sparsely furnished room, like I said, but it doesn't seem empty. Or rather, it seems the room of someone who knows the uses and value of empty space. It somehow reminds me of the Orient or what I imagine the Orient to be. There are no pictures on the wall, nor even tapestries. It's as if she has everything needful already inside herself. It seems, in other words, the room of someone who looks inward. But the cleanliness is the main surprise, and only one lone spiderweb in a high corner, like a string of almost invisible jewels. There is an old-fashioned Victrola and a pile of records. I notice something by Louis Armstrong.

"I don't see any herbs and potions," I observe, standing in the middle of the room.

"I keep my herbs and potions in the kitchen. My teas and candies. You can make healthy candies out of the right combinations of plants and herbs. How can I help you? Are you looking for a root tea? What ailment did you come with?"

"I don't come with an ailment; I come with a question."

"You weren't looking like you come with an ailment. But sometimes a question can be an ailment, can't it, sir?"

I tell her about the Unicorn Woman.

"Well, she needs to come here herself and not to send you. I have to see her before I can recommend a cure to her."

"She didn't send me. I came here actually to ask you whether the horn is real or not. Whether such a thing can actually exist in the world."

"It can be real, but I would have to see it and test it, and then I would assume that she'd want it cured, like I said. All I can tell you now, after hearing your story, is that it *could* be real. Things that I've seen make me suspect that it is, but you'd have to bring the woman to me. I'd have to see her for myself. Do you think you'd be able to bring her here?"

"I don't believe so. Not yet. Anyway, I'm not sure she'd want it cured."

"Her or you?"

I say nothing. That's when I glance at the title I'd originally misread as *Baffling Island*. Baffin Island. How would a baffled island feel?

Then I explain the horn: that the Unicorn Woman is a carnival act and that she needs the horn in her profession. Miss Leeds looks as if that doesn't make any real difference to her way of figuring things.

"Well, while you're here, do you want me to give you something for the stomach trouble you got?"

"I didn't say anything about stomach trouble."

"I know you didn't. You didn't have to tell me. You're talking about things of the heart, or the spirit, and I tell you about the stomach. I know my business. I'll go in here and get you a little garlic oil. Won't even charge you for it."

"Oh, I'll pay you, Miss Leeds. How much do you charge?"

"You already paid me by telling me about somebody I didn't even know existed in the world. I once cured a callus on a little girl's forehead that she got from knocking her little head against the wall all the time, but I've never cured a horn. I'd like to try that. Maybe that's all it is anyway, just some new kind of overgrown callus, and the carnival people mistake it or advertise it for a horn."

She brings me the garlic oil and I thank her. She also gives me some peppermint tea.

"You can thank me again when you win that unicorn woman, if you bring her here and let me see her, even if she doesn't want to be cured. I'd just like to see her for myself."

I don't reply.

"Uh, do you want me to put a little piece of paper on this bottle to identify what it is and what it's for? And the tea?"

"No, I'll remember."

"Good. I don't believe in wasting paper. Wasting paper is like wasting a tree, at least that's what they tell me."

At first I think she means the conservationists, then I suddenly wonder if she means the trees! She is just the sort of person who would talk to trees. Of course I don't ask her that. I'd always felt uncomfortable around that kind of talk, and around mystical people and people who talked to plants and trees.

I say thanks again and get in my car. Smell of honeysuckles, black walnut. She waves. A hummingbird hovers in the honeysuckle bush, flying backwards, then sideways, then hovering again over a flower. Aren't they the only birds that can fly backwards? I wave at Miss Leeds, then head straight.

A midget—do they say "tiny person" these days?—kneels in front of a tin basin washing a man's feet, scrubbing his long ruddy toes with a miniature hairbrush. I watch the tiny person but not the man. The man I watch only from the corners of my eyes. Reared back in a brown swivel desk chair, he sits right-angled to an oak secretary, puffing a cigar. Facing the tiny person, he doesn't look at me. His profile resembles Disraeli's.

Papers scatter the desktop. The frothy water smells like borax and twenty mules. An uncapped and half-empty bottle of impure-looking mineral oil rests beside the basin. The little person raises off his knees and squats, leaning forward slightly, scrubbing vigorously. The trailer is cluttered with carnival paraphernalia: multicolored thingamajigs that you can't identify by name.

"If I let every guy who got passionate about her see her, I couldn't run a carnival," says the owner. "And it ain't just her. There's the Crocodile Woman and of course there's your traditional Bearded Lady. Fellows all the time want to see those dames, up close and personal, if you know what I mean. In fact, another passionate jokester was in here just ahead of you, mister, asking about the same dame and claiming to be a professor of hornicology at some university, or some nonsense and thought it gave him special privileges. A real jokester. I don't understand that sort of passion myself. Don't understand it and don't want to understand it. You amorous jokesters take the cake. And there are a lot of lunatics in the world that get obsessed with these women. I don't know who's a jokester and who's a lunatic. You might be either. And some folks just don't like me for allowing the colored folks into my carnival and because I don't discriminate. I figure this is a new day and age."

The little man is slender, not stocky like some of the little men you see, he looks like a little boy. They are both wearing dungarees.

"If I let every fellow who wanted to see Ziggy see Ziggy, I wouldn't be in the carnival business, you know what I mean, bud? I'd be in another business. And I wouldn't be the boss."

The little man wipes the man's feet and rubs them gently with mineral oil.

"Even Mr. Masters here is fond of Ziggy, ain't you?" The little man says nothing.

"I don't understand that kind of passion myself. Do you, Mr. Masters?"

The little man shakes his head but looks as if he understands perfectly.

I stand and watch the Unicorn Woman and wait for her revolving high stool to revolve toward me. It's a stool that not only turns itself, but raises and lowers itself as if it were powered by some type of hydraulic system or power, but there is none visible. One stares across at her, down at her, and up at her. She does not raise or lower her own head, however. She looks as if she's made out of brass, and she has the sort of expression one sees on mannequins, except for an occasional flash of an indescribable expression that lets you know she has a spirit in the brass. Of what nature or blend of natures she is, I'm still uncertain. I wonder if she's noticed that I've made my appearance several times and whether she thinks I'm an obsessed man, a jokester or a lunatic?

I've come with a prepared question: Were you born with a horn, or did it just grow and when? I don't ask. I've thought also to ask simply, What's your name? But that would have been a dishonest question since I already knew her name. That is, if the owner of the carnival was a truth teller and not just a jokester himself.

People in the milling crowd ask each other questions, but no one addresses questions to the Unicorn Woman herself, not even: Is that a real horn? Then she'd have to answer yes, wouldn't she?

———————

"Blanche's a drama teacher, did I tell ya?" Grange is saying. "I always tell her, if I didn't know what she taught in the classroom I could always tell, because she's got these very expressive features, just like theatrical people, and her hair always looks like it's wet, like somebody pasted wet feathers all over her head. Ya know what I mean?"

"Sure."

"I'll tell you what I learned Sunday, not just artsy-craftsy stuff either.

"Blanche is well-rounded. For one thing, I learned the universe is either expanding or contracting, but no one knows for sure which. And when there's a new moon, the moon is invisible. That explains those nights I couldn't find a moon. That's the difference between the full moon and the new moon. The new moon's invisible; the full moon's completely visible. When I asked Blanche what made that so, she didn't say. Still, it's an interesting bit of information. And it explains those nights when I can't find a moon. Blanche is the type of person who goes about teaching everybody everything you can imagine, or the store of information that she knows.

"You know those types of people, don't you, Bud?"

As soon as I open the door of the trailer, the man, still in profile, says, "You back gain, dreamer? Go hunt passion somewhere else, will ya?"

The little man, staring at me full-faced and rubbing his hands together, says, "I love a good love story. And this is a mystery too, eh?"

"Just make sure you do your job, Mr. Masters," says the carnival boss. "Leave the mysterious abysmal zones to them that's in the business."

The dream leaps, changing scenes, and suddenly I'm sitting in a bar in Paducah, Kentucky. The Unicorn Woman, dressed up to resemble Carmen Miranda, wears a bowl of fruit on her head and a necklace of bananas, passion fruit, and pineapple rings. She's dancing and prancing near my table.

"Do you like my hat?" she asks.

"I adore it."

Her protruding belly button, speckled with glitter, looks almost like a miniature horn itself.

"How do you like Paducah?"

"I love it, but you'd be anywhere and I'd love it. You know that."

"I have to keep moving you know, because I'm in danger."

"What sort of danger?"

"Men keep following me around. Passion, you know. Least the carnival boss says it's that. He says it's passion, but I'm not sure myself. Me, I don't know the difference between passion and curiosity."

"Curiosity is a part of passion. Passion is the foundation of curiosity, or curiosity is the foundation of passion."

"Say what? Are you a schoolteacher? Well, whether it is passion or curiosity that fascinates the people, it's the horn, not me. It represents something for 'em. To tell you the truth, this horn just grew. Woke up one morning and there it was, just like a new moon. It just grew, like Topsy's."

I explain to her the difference between a new moon and a full moon.

Her horn, therefore, has to be a full moon.

"Is that right? Well, you learn something every day, don't you? Thanks a million, Bud. Well, I've got to run."

"Where to next?"

"I just follow the carnival, Bud. I just follow the carnival. It's a traveling carnival. If some nice gent could propose a vision of my horn that I liked, I might follow *him*."

I try to propose a vision of her horn to her, a vision that she might like, but I awake inside a new dream.

"I think she's an angel come to dwell among us," says a woman.

"Or a devil," says the man she's with.

"Her name's Zigagiz. You can read it backwards or forwards and it's the same."

"Sounds like a devil's name to me."

"Or an angel's."

"Zigagiz Dalanalad."

"Didn't I tell you? No ordinary human woman. Ordinary human women don't have names like that."

The Unicorn Woman rotates till she blurs. When she comes into focus again, the horn is gone.

"Just an ordinary human woman," says the woman. "Didn't I say so? Without that horn, she's the same as you or me."

I drive the tractor out to the Hennebelle farm. It's one of those farms that lets you know how bluegrass got its name and why it deserves it: the grass is so green it looks blue. Cows and horses graze in one swollen meadow. In another, corn, wheat, and barley are planted. Another is reserved for tobacco, its leaves undulating. The farm is surrounded by a rock fence, each stone of individual character, shape, and color laid individually perhaps five generations ago, the sort of fence that hardly needs mending. I imagine the old days and slaves mending the fence, watched by an overseer. Somebody said slave cabins are still on this property, but I haven't seen them myself. I've only traveled on the outskirts of the property, along the borderline, and they say the slave cabins are inward. But I imagine those old slaves hand-placing the stones meticulously. In fact, everything on the farm looks hand-placed, as if an architect's and landscapist's scale model, magically enlarged and brought to life. The Hennebelle mansion, Jeffersonian, sits half a mile back from the road. It is white with a multitude of tiny, green-framed windows.

Hennebelle could be peeking out of any of them, observing me. I imagine him as the master in the old days and me one of the retainers. Why do I think "retainer" and not just slave? Then I imagine myself a slave on loan or rented from one of the other plantations, a skilled craftsman. I think one of my ancestors was a blacksmith who used to travel from plantation to plantation. Momentarily, I think I see a man standing in one of the windows, in shirtsleeves, holding a pipe, but it's the flickering shadows of an elm.

I've seen Hennebelle only once in person—a short white man with his straight red hair combed forward like an umbrella bird's feathers—a quick glance while he pranced by on horseback while I was returning another tractor. He nodded to me and I nodded to him. We did not exchange words. He continued to prance on. I saw him another time, though, in the society pages of the *Lexington Herald-Leader*: his hair combed back from his broad forehead this time but still longer than it was stylish to wear in those days. He looked more like someone from another century. Forward or backward, I wasn't sure. He could have been from the nineteenth century, or he could have been from some future century. Dressed in white tie and white tails, in the newspaper photo, he did not look like a bird of any variety. His ears peeking up between the bushy blades of his hair. His pretty wife beside him wore black fur.

They had four handsome sons standing nearby wearing little jockey costumes: Josh, Wilde, Stern, and Clever. Years later I read in the same newspaper that son Josh, the eldest, had had a play produced on Broadway or Off-Broadway and that it had made him a sensation in certain New York literary circles. The local paper had reprinted some of the reviews, three of which I still remember:

"This is a wild, impertinent, spiritual comedy. J. H. is a new theatrical sensation."

"J. H. is a pleasantly sardonic prophet of our modern age. Bravo!"

"This is a play of irredeemable vulgarity: vulgarity of thought, of character, of sentiments, of language. It does not belong on or off the Great White Way."

I believe it was the latter critic that Josh Hennebelle must have listened to, because I read no further notices of plays, on or off Broadway or even locally, written by Josh "Henny" Hennebelle. I did read a small item about him a decade later, that he had roamed from New York to Amsterdam to New Guinea, then he'd become the assistant manager in an upstate New York office paper products company. He was about to marry the former Miss Thala Kodiak Arctos of New York City, who was photographed in a white fur coat, in the days when society women always wore furs. The caption underneath her read "Venus in Furs." Perhaps this caption struck her fancy because the new Mrs. Josh Hennebelle was said to be a bit of an eccentric who insisted upon wearing fur both summer and winter, indeed every season.

Of the other Hennebelle boys, Wilde stayed on the farm and married his childhood sweetheart. Camera shy, he never appeared on the society pages. Stern became a horse breeder and stayed a bachelor, though he is often photographed with Hollywood and Las Vegas showgirls visiting Kentucky for the Derby, and every Kentucky Derby Stern throws a gigantic Derby Day party, photographs of which take up several society pages. Recipes of dishes served there, such as "Cantaloupe Chocolate Mousse Delight," are reprinted for local housewives. Party guests descend from helicopters and step out of pontoon boats. There's usually a surprise celebrity guest of honor.

I don't remember reading any notices about Clever. Once, out of curiosity, I attempted to ask one of the hired men at the Hennebelle farm what had become of Clever, but he didn't understand me. So I'm not certain that his name truly is Clever or whether that was a newspaper misspelling of the name.

One of the Hennebelles, while visiting Hawaii, was overheard to have said that the native Hawaiians looked like Negroes too much for her taste. Except it wasn't the word "Negro" she was reported to have said but the more derogatory name. "They may call them Hawaiians, but they look like N_____ to me." I suppose she had seen too many Hawaiians in the movies played by white people or colored people of other nationalities. J. A. Rogers, in one of his books, was reported to have overheard a similar comment from a Caucasian visitor to the islands.

"How you doing, Bud?" asks Putman, one of the hired men, who appears as soon as I park the tractor inside the gate. When Putman calls my name I can never tell whether he's calling me out of my name or calling me by name.

I climb down from the tractor and give him the invoice. "Do you use?" he asks, offering me a tin of snuff.

"No thanks."

He pinches a bit and snuffs.

"I don't know, Bud," he says, putting a dab more under his tongue, snapping the tin shut and putting it in his shirt pocket. "I think the land just don't like a machine. I think it rebels. Mr. Hennie's making a fuss over this one tractor, though, like he thinks it's a sacred tractor. I think either the land don't like a machine or the machine don't like the land. Gotta be one or the other. Do you want a cup of coffee while you're waiting for your ride? Come up to the kitchen."

"No thanks. I'll just wait here by the rock fence."

"Okey dokey, suit yourself, mister. Don't get me wrong. I'm not talking against the machine, even a sacred machine. I believe in the machine myself. I worked on 'em during the war. But it's got to be something. Grange brought this tractor in the last time, so I know y'all ain't playing tricks on us. Well, see you around, Bud. I hope it ain't on the same tractor, though."

He laughs, showing discolored but marvelously well-shaped teeth, gums pink but spotted with flecks of brown. He has a wide mouth and an overbite, which makes him look like those museum reconstructions of an early version of man. He reminds me of someone I've seen in the movies—old cowboy movies. His straight brown hair looks like it was cut under a bowl. He climbs upon the tractor and drives into a long shed where other farm equipment and farm machines are kept. He doesn't exit, so I assume he has work to do inside.

I stand against the rock fence thinking of rebel land or rebellious land and light a Philip Morris cigarette. A Hennebelle goat, grazing in a nearby meadow, suddenly rushes for the rock fence, charging, then stops short and lazily chews and watches me.

"So what do you think about the horn, fella? Do you think it's as real as your own?"

I study his horn. It really does seem manufactured of the same stuff as the Unicorn Woman's. But real horns are supposed to have a center of bone. I wonder if hers has a center of bone. I suppose *his* does.

"What advice would you give? Are you any kin to the unicorn, even if it is a mythical beast? What do you know about your cousin? What's your advice?"

Of course he gives no advice but looks as if he's got plenty to give, however nonchalantly, if one could only comprehend goat vocabulary. He continues to chew. What do three consecutive, rapid chews mean, then one, pause, then a long, slow, languorous, solemn chew?

"Cigarette?"

A shake of the beard. Well, that's understandable in any language.

But he looks at me like I'm an articulate machine.

A tender chestnut colt grazing farther up in the meadow eating green seems to be almost wading in green, wind tossing its forelock like a bohemian's. Rigid brown haystacks rise nearby, the sun peeking around them as if they were a straw man's shoulders. Watching the colt, I think of Colorado or Wyoming or one of the Dakotas, but the West has always seemed to me like one big state. I think of once reading about black cowboys out west, maybe some historical book or something, again, by J. A. Rogers. Cowboys you never see in the Western movies. I try to remember the name of a black town out west they settled. Boley, Colorado? Even horses native to Kentucky always remind me of the West. Of rodeos, not the Derby. I think of the black freetowns in Kentucky, founded by former slaves. Once I had started to take a tour of the freetowns. A photographer from the North had come to Kentucky to photograph them.

Cars whisk by, trucks, then a solitary tractor lumbers down the road.

A small, fleet dairy truck marked "Gulliver Ulysses Waterhouse's Dairy" turns in at the gate. The dairyman, who is probably not Gulliver but a hired man, does not drive up to the house but goes to the corner of the hip-roofed barn where he deposits, beside a rusty water pump, a case of milk bottles and retrieves the empty ones. As he drives back, I catch a glimpse of him through the wide windshield glass: he has the broad, high-cheekboned face of a man I met once overseas who said he was from the Sandwich Islands, a brown-skinned man, but this one is as pale as the milk truck or the goat's beard. Still he has the same features of the Sandwich Islands man. He does not glance my way but stares obliviously forward, as the truck heads for the exit, adding to the jungle of tracks in the grayish brown dust. Ellison had not yet written *Invisible Man*. But that's how I feel: like an invisible man. But I can smell my armpits like wet hay as I raise my arms trying to escape the flying dust.

Another truck, a cleaner's delivery truck, pauses in front of the gate; the driver looks for a moment as if he can't remember the gate or does not know the proper gate. He examines a chart, then drives on. Somewhere, unseen, I hear water running over rock. A hidden stream somewhere in the distance. If there wasn't a "no trespassing" sign posted on the gate, I'd go hunt for it. And maybe hunt for the slave cabins too. There is no shade, and in the bold sunlight, I'm sweating like a river. I feel like I'm made of oil and tar. Suddenly I feel too visible.

The goat, still keeping me company, chews, indifferent. Then he chews, observing me, observing the highway, observing Ranch, as he drives up in the pickup truck and toots the horn. I spit out the butt end of my cigarette, stamp it out, and climb in.

"Were you talking to that goat?" asks Ranch.

"Yeah. Wanted his advice on a matter."

"What advice did he give you?"

"Not a thing."

"Sign of true wisdom," says Ranch, without a word more.

———————————

The Carmen Miranda hat, but the Unicorn Woman's not under it. It's thrown among the other carnival paraphernalia. The little man, sitting on the pile of junk sculpture, watches me.

"You again? Human Befriending Goat Befriender Bearing Questions? Well, I've got a question for you. Suppose she were a rhino woman or an antelope woman? Would you still be fascinated by her?"

I think of African women, then I think of Native American women, but I don't reply to his question. I do, however, like his new name for me.

"Here we are," says Ranch, turning in the gate of the tractor repair company. "Did you have a good nap?"

I say, "Thanks," climb down, and take the invoice to the office.

Peggy, the secretary, blonde hair in a pompadour, stamps the invoice, separates the pieces, the original and the two carbons, in three different gray metal trays, then hands me the fourth carbon. A spit curl dangling in the middle of her forehead softens the effect of the pompadour.

Her lips are tiny and pink, but her eyes are huge, close-set, and parrot-green. She's younger than she looks. In those days, young women tried to look older. In these days, old women try to look younger. I remember when I first came there to work, she'd shown some alarm that the company had hired a colored man as a tractor repairman. She didn't seem to know how to treat or react to me. But she's gotten used to seeing me around, though I don't stay around her too long. I just hand in my invoices and exit.

Out back, Grange looks up, a wrench in his hand.

"You back? Almost quitting time. Y'all should've just taken y'all's time driving back, you and Ranch. Start on the new tractor tomorrow."

Grange hadn't taken his time getting back. I wonder why he'd advised me to do what he hadn't done. But maybe he thinks I don't like tractor fixing as much as he does. He's one of those tractor fixers who even fixes tractors in his spare time, maybe even in his dreams, like somebody said actors on holiday always went to see a play. A tractor fixer's tractor fixer.

"Well, I'll just look 'er over, see what's to be done," I say.

"Always too much," says Grange. "If folks knew how to treat a tractor, we wouldn't have to work so hard. A machine needs tender loving care, same as a woman. That's how you treat a machine. Of course not too tender, or they won't do their job, right? Or like those science fiction stories about machines taking control of the world."

I walk around the tractor, climb up on it, start it, listen, climb down.

"You look kinda dreamy," he says. "What're you dreaming about? Memphis?"

"Yeah."

"Always Memphis. Musta been a real doll, that woman, whoever she is. I've seen some of those Memphis women myself. Real beauties. They're not as beautiful as Kentucky women, though, but they've got their own brand of beauty. A man don't turn into a Memphian for nothing."

I say nothing. Memphian. Sounds like a religion. Like you could make a religion of a place. Unicornian. What would that be? I think of the saying about Kentucky: land of fast horses and beautiful women. Of course, some people make a joke of it and say "land of fast women and beautiful horses."

Like you could make a religion of a woman? Hadn't I read that somewhere? Where a man made a religion of a woman?

"I don't know," says Grange, as I tinker with the tractor. "I think you ought to watch out for those women that make you a dreamer, though.

"Women that make you a dreamer are never what you expect. Never are what you expect. They never are. They're all illusion and confusion. Now I'm speaking to you from experience, which is the best teacher. Blanche believes you can know some things without experiencing 'em, by looking at pictures and reading books and using the power and persuasiveness of your own imagination. I don't believe it. It don't sound rational. If you don't learn from your own experience, you got to learn from somebody's else's. I mean, somebody that experiences the world directly. Now that's rational.

"And I know where from I speak. Illusion and confusion, that's all it is. Plus, women make you a dreamer while you're courting 'em, but then when you get 'em they keep you wide awake. I know where from I speak. Pick a woman while you're wide awake and you know what you got."

"That sounds like some sound advice," I say, using a trick my Aunt Maggie taught me.

"I know it's sound advice," he says, putting his tools away. "Because I've experienced both kinds of women, the kind you pick when you're dreaming and the kind you choose when you're wide awake. I know where from I speak. I chose my wife when I was wide awake. But some of my girlfriends before her I picked out when I was dreaming."

I take off my greasy gray work jacket and put on my gabardine street jacket and start for the exit. Grange walks along beside me.

"Of course the younger men never listen to an older man when he's talking to him," he says, wiping oily hands on a dirt-black undershirt he uses for a cleaning rag, then stuffing it into his tool box that he carries home with him. Like I said, he fixes tractors in his spare time.

"That's why the men stay backwards when it comes to a woman," he says. "A woman will listen to another woman, I mean even an older woman, and get ahead and learn from her, but a man has always got to be his own. That's why we haven't progressed. I mean, we've made mechanical and technological progress, but on the subject of the woman we haven't progressed at all. Plus, the womenfolk have developed their faculty of intuition and men seem to fear intuition and the tenderer things of the mind and the spirit. With womenfolk those things are a priority."

At the gate, he asks, "Did you see Kate peeking at you?"

"Kate?"

"Yeah, Kate Riley. She's the woman they had working here, fixing tractors when the men were off fighting the war. You know they hired a lot of womenfolk to do the work of the men. So our company hired Kate. Fired her when the men came back, and then they hired you, and also you being a colored man and all, I suppose that got Kate Riley riled up."

This is the first time he's mentioned me being a colored man, almost as if he's just noticing the fact. Otherwise he's been treating me like he doesn't notice color. I'm just another tractor repairman.

"No, I didn't notice," I say.

"Well, she notices you. She's always walking by here looking mad as a wet hen. Well, it's as much her fault as anybody's. They offered to put her in the office along with Peggy—I call her Pompadour Peggy—but she wouldn't go. She said that would be a waste of her talents. That she was fixing tractors all throughout the war and she could fix them better now. But it seems like it would be a move up if you ask me, but she didn't see it that way. She treated it like they were demoting her. They even said she could be employed polishing the tractors, once we men repaired them, but she didn't take that opportunity either. The boss gave her freedom of choice.

"When you're free to choose, that makes you responsible. I don't see why she didn't pick tractor polisher if she was so keen on tractors. Polish up the tractors when we men got through fixing them; that's a real nice upwardly mobile job. I try to see her part, but a man back from the war wants his job back. You fought in the war, so you need your job back the same as any man. Don't matter to me what's your color; you're still a tractor fixer. And a pretty good one to my lights. We even had her daddy talk to her. He's the man who does the topiary work you see around here for the people that don't like their bushes and trees to be natural but want them carved into animals and birds and pyramids and such. Mr. Pinxit wanted her daddy to trim a bush to look like a duck. That's what topiary work is. A right nice little business he's got for himself. She wouldn't even listen to her daddy.

"Some women are like that. They've got to be their own women. Her daddy's a man of all work, though, not just a topiary man, so she should have listened to him. But if you see a woman peeking in here looking like a wet hen, that's Kate Riley. Even Peggy talked to her, woman to woman, you know, and confidentially, but she won't listen. Women are forward in love and the tender things, but sometimes they can be backwards and bullheaded in everything else."

I say nothing.

"The next time I see Kate Riley I will explain to her that you didn't take her job from her, that you had this job before the war, and got it fair and square. I didn't know they hired any colored fellows to work here before the war, but the boss says you usedta come up here as a youngster and fix tractors, even before my time. And he let you learn the business. I don't really think of you as being colored myself. The little Kentucky town I'm from you couldn't tell white from colored, because we all looked the same. It's in our history. Outsiders couldn't tell, but we all knew each other. We knew who was who. We knew who was colored and who was white. Outsiders were always amazed at us. Even the sheriff of the county couldn't tell the difference. Sometimes he would lock up a colored man when he thought he was locking up a white man and sometimes he would lock up a white man when he thought he was locking up a colored man and put them in the wrong segregated cell. Even though we could tell who was colored and who was white and we'd try to warn him. But sometimes the colored was whiter than the white. And sometimes the white was more colored than the colored. That's just the history of the place. I just think of you as another tractor fixer. Kate'll pull in her horns after a while. She won't cause no trouble. Riley raised her right."

Outside, he heads in one direction and I another. I try to picture his little town.

Going to my parked car, I pass Peggy, standing at the bus stop. She pretends not to notice me.

"Tell us your name."

"Kate."

"A real universal name. I didn't think it was Ziga. Here you have 'em, gents: the Parrot Woman, the Chameleon Woman, the Unicorn Woman, the Bearded Lady. Take your pick. Pay an extra dime for the Bearded Lady and we'll even allow you to do topiary work. How does that grab ya?"

I pay to go see the Parrot Woman. She smiles in front of me, but not at me.

"Polly Pompadour's my name," she says. "Or Pompadour Polly. What's your game?" When I don't answer, she pouts and asks, "Do you want a cracker?"

I drive Aunt Maggie to see the woman she calls Doc Leeds. "Why don't you drive around a little bit," says Aunt Maggie, as we enter Midway's city limits. "I never do like to catch that woman listening to *Amos 'n' Andy*. I don't mind *Perry Mason* or the *Orson Welles Commentaries*, which she sometimes will listen to. Or the radio romances. But she will stop in the midst of treating you to listen to *Amos 'n' Andy*.

"I've experienced that. I don't see why colored people find them so humorous. They're an embarrassment to the race. I wish there was a colored *Perry Mason*. Or a colored *Quiz Kids* or a colored *The Shadow* or other of the radio shows and radio series. Or even a colored radio romance. But that *Amos 'n' Andy* . . . I don't understand how intelligent people like Doc Leeds can listen to them and love them. She behaves like she loves them. Like she really loves them and finds them hilarious. I guess there are some people that are closet *Amos 'n' Andy* listeners among our race. Do you listen to *Amos 'n' Andy*?"

She looked at me as if whether or not one listened to *Amos 'n' Andy* was a judgment of character.

"Sometimes."

"Well, at least you're honest. Some people ain't even honest. I prefer *The Romance of Helen Trent* myself. I would like it even better if it were a colored man and woman. A romance between a colored man and woman, but they wouldn't put that on the radio. Not in this day and age."

We cross Railroad Street. As we cross the tracks, she bounces into my shoulder, says excuse me, and straightens up.

"I remember on V-J Day everybody was dancing out here on Railroad Street. Everybody. Dancing in the street. Men, women, children, white, colored, and one Indian. You know Mr. Dancing, don't you? The Indian man? He was out here. He wasn't dancing." She chuckles. "He was watching. A few got drunk and pretended like they was Indians. Hahjo hahjo hahjo. That's the sound they was making. I don't know if that's a true Indian sound. I don't know if the Indian people really sound like that or if it's just for the movies. I never like to see people do that. Play Indian, you know. I don't like to see people play Indian any more than I like the minstrel shows. Mr. Dancing just watched them. He watched all of them.

"He was even watching the colored people, because there were some colored people playing Indian. And me, I stood there watching Mr. Dancing. But every time I see Railroad Street I think of V-J Day. I think of the war being over, and I think of you returning from the war. I think of people dancing in the street and I think of Mr. Dancing. I will. Well, I will say I trust Doc Leeds on just about every matter, except for *Amos 'n' Andy* and her preference for that radio show. You haven't had any more problems with your stomach, have you?"

"As a matter of fact, I haven't."

"And you won't. Because Dr. Leeds knows her business. A little knowledge is a dangerous thing, she's always saying, but she has more than a little knowledge."

We park on Railroad Street in front of a men's clothing store. I light up a cigarette.

"You ought to have Doc Leeds talk to you about internal pollution," says Aunt Maggie. "You wouldn't smoke cigarettes anymore."

I smoke anyway.

As we pull up in front of Doc Leeds's, she's turning off the radio.

"I know you; you're the Unicorn Hunter," she says, pointing at me, as we step onto the porch.

"How do, Maggie?"

I sit in the wicker chair on the porch while Aunt Maggie goes into the parlor. I can hear them through the open window to the right of me.

"Why don't you give me a little bit of everything, Dr. Leeds?"

"Now you know I can't do that, Mag. Some combinations of things don't go well with others. You just stick to your regimen."

"The program you put Golgi Tatum on, she says makes her hair grow."

"Now you know I cannot put everyone on the same regimen, because you're all individual people, but if you're worried about your hair, I can give you something to make it grow. This is made with peanuts, so you will have to mix a little brilliantine or a little sweet oil in with it to camouflage the smell. Rub it into your scalp and a little bit on your hair. It will also make it glisten and shine."

"I know what you gave Golgi makes her hair real healthy. I like healthy hair. And Golgi told me you also gave her something made with oysters."

"That was not for her hair, Mag. You think you can go around asking other people what I give them, and it will work for you. Everybody is an individual and needs a customized and personalized regimen. What works for Golgi might not work for you, Maggie. You just stick to your own regimen and don't worry about Golgi's regimen."

"I wish you had something that could make a person remember what they want to remember and forget all the stuff they want to."

"The memory is impartial."

"Well, it seems pretty partial to me. Partial to what you want to forget."

"I can give you something for mental clarity."

"Yes, I need me some mental clarity."

"Well, I'll go back in here and get your medicaments."

Silence. I watch the chickens. One marches a bit ahead of the others, looking like a scout. Smell of honeysuckles, black walnut, milkweed. I listen to the eternal hum of the country. From inside, the clink of jars, then the crisp crack of paper. If one destroys trees to make paper, what does one destroy to make glass?

"Here you are."

"I wish you would just give me a little bit of everything though. What won't cure one thing will cure something else."

"That ain't the way it works, Mag. You just stick to your own regimen. Put a little bit in your scalp at night before you brush your hair. If you heat it first, it works even better. Also, put a half teaspoon of this in your cup of coffee or whatever you imbibe in the morning."

"Chamomile tea."

"Say what?"

"What I imbibe in the morning."

"Good for you. You oughta try ginger tea and peppermint tea."

"I would like to try some of that oyster stuff too, Doc Leeds. Fedora Doppler said she got some oyster stuff too, and I know I have got the same constitution as Fedora."

"Now, Mag, there are no two people that have the same constitution. They may resemble each other. You might resemble Fedora Doppler, but you're not her. And having the same constitution is an illusion. If you think you need some oyster stuff, go buy yourself some oysters. You just got a fixation on oysters. Go home and make yourself an oyster casserole or some oyster stew."

Aunt Maggie is silent, then she says, "Doc Leeds, I heard somebody say she slept with a magnet under her pillow. Does that make the hair grow and make it healthy?"

"Ptah! Fiddlesticks!"

They're back on the porch and Aunt Maggie is sticking a bag into her pocketbook. She rummages in it, then snaps it shut. Her pocketbook looks like the cheeks of a fat, greedy brown squirrel. She takes a few dollars from her purse and puts them in Doc Leeds's hands. Doc Leeds returns some of the money.

"You are worth your hire," says Aunt Maggie, or something similar.

"Don't forget when you find your Unicorn Woman I'd like to see her," Doc Leeds says to me.

"I've already found her; I just don't have her," I say, rising.

"You haven't found her till you've got her," she says.

"If the carnival comes back this way, I'll let you know," I say.

"I don't like to go to carnivals or circuses either," says Doc Leeds. "They disturb my spirit."

I wait for her to say more, but she doesn't. We wave so long. I hold the car door for Aunt Maggie and she gets in.

"*Amos 'n' Andy* ought to disturb her spirit," mumbles Aunt Maggie as we drive off. "They ought to disturb the spirit of the race. They are portrayed by white men pretending to be colored people. It is not unlike a minstrel show, except on the radio."

"Did you get everything you need?" I ask.

"Everything I need, but not everything I want," says Aunt Maggie.

"Suppose what you want harms you?" I ask.

"An oyster never harmed nobody," says Aunt Maggie. "Except maybe another oyster. I guess I could make myself an oyster casserole or some oyster stew."

We cross Spring Station Bridge.

"Drive back by Railroad Street," says Aunt Maggie. "I want to remember when the war was over. Everybody was out there dancing except Mr. Dancing." She giggles like a young girl. "He did have a sip of my Thunderbird, though. I have danced with him at Tiger's Inn. That was many years ago, when we were youngsters. But that day, he just watched everybody. He watched everybody, and I watched him. But even colored people were playing Indian. I don't like to see that. We should be better behaved than that. But Mr. Dancing was watching everybody. He is still a handsome and remarkable man."

Instead of driving back to Lexington, we head for Versailles, Kentucky, since we're in the neighborhood, and go by Sam and Sal's Place, which is a restaurant owned by my parents. (Incidentally, Versailles, Kentucky, is not pronounced like the French city but is pronounced the way it's spelled, as if it were "Ver-sails.") Anyway, at Sam and Sal's Place, my father, Sam, is the cook and my mother, Sal, is the waitress, bartender, and cashier. My father's more introverted and cerebral; my mother, more outward and friendly with folks, so she prefers to be where all the people are and also likes to listen to their conversations.

My parents have had the restaurant for about a decade and a half, but I remember stories about before they opened it. Though I was old enough to remember its beginnings more directly, I've always been the sort to remember things more pristinely through stories and storytelling even when I've actually been there. The things that take place in other people's heads and that come to you through stories have always held a special interest for me. I'm an admirer of storytelling and storytellers. I enjoy the spoken revelation. Even if you're like Ella Tallent, a neighborhood woman, who claims to read thoughts, even she reads thoughts in the form of stories, or so she claims. Otherwise, she says people's thoughts are too nebulous or maybe "fogbound."

But to get back to what I was saying. For instance, my father is always saying that the only reason they serve liquor is out of stubbornness. Originally they were just going to serve food and soft drinks, but around the same time that my father was contemplating opening a restaurant, the church we belonged to was contemplating making him a deacon. So the other deacons had a meeting with my father and one of them declared, "Brother Guy, a little bird told us that you are contemplating starting a restaurant."

In those days, and maybe even nowadays, when you didn't want to reveal who told you something, it was acceptable and even expected to say that "a little bird told you." Therefore, when I was small and couldn't distinguish sounds from meanings, I used to think they were accusing someone who carried my name, or maybe even accusing me of tale bearing. You see, often people would pronounce "bird" like "bud." So it sounded to me like they were saying, "A little bud told me." Finally, when I was able to distinguish that "bird" pronounced "bud" was still "bird," I used to picture a little bird standing in a hollyhock bush or on a golden branch or in a palm tree or on the edge of space with shining feathers. People would come to this little bird like some sort of oracle to be told things. Then, when I discovered Miss Ella Tallent, mentioned above, I thought she'd been that eternal little bird.

"Yes," replied my father. "I'm contemplating starting my own restaurant. What that little *bird* told you is the truth."

(People who have a little "bud" of their own are careful to articulate *bird*. Most of the time they don't pronounce it "bud.")

"The reason we called you to council, Brother Guy," the deacon went on, "is that we are contemplating making you a deacon of the church, and we don't feel it would be commendable or look right either for a deacon of the church to be an owner of a din of iniquity and to be serving liquor and strong intoxicating drinks."

I believe it was Eland Cohune who spoke, being the head and eldest deacon, but I wasn't present, so I can't be certain. The other deacons who were present were Chatter Randan and Frosh Dunn. Chatter Randan seldom had a word to say to anybody; hence, his name. They always referred to him as "Chatterbox," but I believe Chatter was his true name.

Frosh Dunn believed in the principle of affirming a truth once someone else had spoken it, so I'm pretty certain it was Eland Cohune who was the spokesman. However, whenever my father retells the story, he only admits to "one of the deacons."

My father insisted that it was a restaurant he was contemplating opening and not a "din of iniquity."

"But you'll serve liquor and strong and intoxicating drinks, and that will contribute to sin as well as alcoholism," the deacon asserted. "And when people drink they also smoke and dance, which are equally iniquitous, till one sin leads them to another and you don't know how many sins people will contemplate. If that's not a 'din of iniquity' I don't know what is. It's an honor to be made a deacon, Brother Guy, even to have it proposed to you, and you are a well-respected member of the church and the congregation and always have been, but if you open a din of iniquity, we wouldn't be able to honor you with deaconhood."

Therefore, it was actually the deacons of our church who were responsible for my father's opening the restaurant and serving strong and intoxicating drinks, and even having a jukebox. But, of course, he was never made a deacon.

Out of further stubbornness, my father had started to "signify" by naming his restaurant "The Deacon," but my mother persuaded him not to because after all they were still a part of the church community even if they were not officers of the church, so he named it "Sam and Sal's Place."

When we arrive, my mother is behind the counter polishing glasses and my father is sitting at a window table with a newspaper and a Coke. I go get a Coke, sit down across from my father, and he passes me the sports section. Mr. Humphrey Sable, a local barber, peeks in the window and waves, says, "Hoo there," or what sounds like "Hoo there." Aunt Maggie sits up at the counter drinking rum and talking to my mother.

"I don't know why," says Aunt Maggie. "I'm just nervous all the time. You know how you get nervous all the time? I'm as nervous as a flycatcher."

"I don't know what a flycatcher is, but I know what you mean."

"I don't believe that a woman has to go through two changes, do you?"

My mother stops polishing glasses and looks like she's polishing thumbs.

"No, I believe there's only one change. Of course, there's a change in the beginning, during puberty. But they don't refer to that as a change."

"I believe there's only one change, and I've been through that. Doc Leeds has only heard of one change, and she should know."

"That's the truth."

"When I was going through the change, Doc Leeds was the only one who had medicaments that could help me. She prepared me some sort of tea and told me what foods I should and shouldn't eat. She made me something with cucumbers and something with flaxseeds, and she made me a mixture of pureed fruits and vegetables that I was supposed to mix into soups and stews and baked goods. And she gave me little exercises I was supposed to do to keep me functioning properly. And when I was having trouble with my crocheting, she gave me some finger exercises to do and some eye exercises. Sometimes she talks to me like I'm a little child, but I tell her I'm not a little child. I'm a grown-up woman. I'm too grown-up. But most of the time she talks like a normal human woman. When I first went to see her, I was expecting something mystical and magical. But there's nothing mystical and magical about her. She's a normal human woman. I know this is not the change."

My father grunts and looks like he has the beginning or the end of a thought but says nothing. He slides the rest of the paper across to me, rises, and heads behind the counter. Reaching down, he brings up clean checkered tablecloths that look freshly ironed and stacked.

"Change these tablecloths; that's something to change," he says.

"A man changes too," says Aunt Maggie. "Doc Leeds says that men change too, and some of them have come to her with their masculine problems. It's not just womenfolk that flock to Doc Leeds. And not just colored people either. She is known far and wide. I don't know if she talks to other people like they're children though. I know that everybody is a child of God."

"You won't get me into your argument," says Father.

"We're not arguing; we're talking" says Mother.

"No, we're not arguing," agrees Aunt Maggie. "Anyway, she gave me some plant-based medicaments from her garden for my new regimen.

"Everything she does is plant-based. And I'm only allowed one rum, straight without the cola. She says I can put a pinch of nutmeg in it. And she believes in the biblical foods: honey, olive oil, cinnamon, and apples. You can make dessert from that. I know they teach you what you shouldn't eat and drink at some people's churches."

My father divides half of the tablecloth with me and we change the tables.

"When y'all drove up," my mother is saying, "Buddy was sort of leaning forward, so we couldn't see anything but your hair. We thought Buddy was bringing his new girlfriend."

"*You* thought buddy was bringing his new girlfriend," corrects my father, straightening a tablecloth. "I knew it was Mag. I can tell Mag's hair."

Aunt Maggie gives a barely perceptible grunt, the kind you only hear if you're listening for it. She has always worried about the length of her hair, though I think she has nice hair.

Heading back, Aunt Maggie says, "I started to tell them about your unicorn woman, but then I wasn't exactly sure whether you'd told them yourself. I figured you'd prefer to tell them yourself."

"No, I haven't mentioned her."

"Shy?"

"I just haven't mentioned her."

"Well, it's a wonder that you mentioned her to me. I was surprised when you actually did go to see Doc Leeds."

We cross Railroad Street again. Crossing the tracks, she bounces up into my shoulder again. "'Scuse me."

"What's Mr. Dancing's first name?" she asks. "I've always known him by Mr. Dancing. Even when he was a youngster, people called him Mister. I once asked him for his first name, but he wouldn't tell me."

I tell her I don't know. Like her, I'd never heard anybody call him anything but Mr. Dancing. Then I remember my father used to call him Dan. I tell her so.

"That's just short for Dancing," she says. "He doesn't like anybody to call him Dance though. I once called him Danny and he allowed it, but I surprised myself. He's a more respectful person than he should be.

"Maybe he's one of those people that don't have a first name. Maybe his full name is Dancing. Maybe he was never given a first name."

"Or maybe he just doesn't want people to know his full name," I say.

"That might be true," says Aunt Maggie. "That might be the truth."

If I reach out to her I can slip her the note with my name and address, and the short comment: "I wish I could get a chance to talk to you." Silly? If I reach out to her and she reaches toward me. If I hurl the note like a rocket and it lands in her lap or near enough for her to spot. If I pick my moment and reach out when no one's looking. But everyone is always looking. We're here to look. If I pick my moment and reach out while everyone's looking but wait till she turns in my direction. Horn of her own invention? And suppose she really did invent that horn herself, then came to the carnival and inquired: "Mister, I've an idea for you. How about 'The Unicorn Woman'? You've got every type of woman, but not a unicorn. I don't think it's been done. It would be unique. I think it would draw a real crowd." Her look is like that of any performer's.

I hold my note tenderly, gingerly at the tips of my nervous fingers. I let it drop when I believe she's looking at me, or at least in my direction. But I must go on belief. I don't hurl it like a rocket, nor do I hand it to her. Rather I just open my fingers and release. I simply let it drop. Perhaps, after the show, she'll pick it up. But her look's like any performer's, and I wonder what she'll do. When you can't go on belief, you go on wonder.

"It's some sin that made it grow," says a man, perhaps a deacon. "Protest your innocence, girl," says another, a rabble rouser type. "Protect your innocence," revises another.

"I think she's divine."

After I let the note drop and release it, I retreat.

When I come to the carnival the next day, the tent is swept clean of debris, but the Unicorn Woman gives no special notice of me. I'm simply a member of the audience, and she's any performer.

"There's such a thing as collective illusion, you know," mumbles a spectator. "I heard something like that on *Orson Welles Commentaries*, or somebody's commentaries."

"She looks really hot to trot to me."

"She'd be difficult to approach though. They guard 'em, you know. They guard and protect them. I've been coming to their carnival since before the war. This is their first unicorn woman. During the Depression, they let some folks get in free."

"Look. It's there. A horn. Incontestable."

"Young woman, have you been baptized?" someone asks. He hands her a note. "This is my church and we're having a revival. I'd like you to attend. And here's the address of the Divine Pilgrim's Church, where I sometimes preach."

So simple? Pretend you're a preacher? Do as you please? Or perhaps he's a real preacher.

I follow the man. He leads me to a real church with a real steeple. I return early that evening and mingle in the multitude. When the door of the church opens, I stay outside. I stand outside the whole of revival week, but no mythical woman enters or leaves. No mystical woman. She had ignored his note. Or perhaps she's just an ordinary woman and the horn isn't real. Inside there are chants of holy passion. Then someone is standing at my elbow. Is this the Divine Pilgrim's Church?

"Hi-de-ho. Son, you've been standing out here all week. I've been watching you, and I'm sure the Holy Spirit's been watching you too. Why don't you come inside and save your soul?"

"I don't know," I admit, shrugging.

"Your soul is yearning; that's why you're here. Your soul is wrestling with you to bring you in. Let your soul win. That's all I can say to you today, son. Let your soul be the victor. That's all I can say to you."

"Thank you, Reverend."

"Don't thank me. Thank your soul that brought you here. And thank the Holy Spirit. I'm just a shepherd of the Lord. Wonders to perform. I am a descendent from preachers from slavery days, with bloodlines all the way back to Africa and before Africa. And we have healers who are descendants of the old-time slaves on the plantations. Some of them are members of our church. Son, there are wonders to perform."

I say nothing. He's holding two books, a Holy Bible and a book in manuscript form called "Appeal for Progress."

"Son, we thought this new war for democracy would mean things would be changing, but the more things change, the more they stay the same. I was a soldier myself, son, and that's what I take you for. They thought I wouldn't go to war because I'm a preacher, but I took up the fight for freedom the same as any man. A fighter for democracy abroad, a warrior and emissary. Some enlisted and some were drafted, but we fought the same war, because we had faith in democracy. We have kept the faith. But it was the same war, the first war, the Great War, and the wars before that. I saw Japanese Americans and Chinese Americans and American Indians and Filipino Americans and Mexican Americans all fighting the same war, doing what soldiers do. . . . We were all soldiers in the same war. . . . We are always fighting on two fronts, and some of us on several fronts. . . . Well, are you coming in, son?"

I stay outside and he returns inside. I can hear him from the church steps. He reads first from the Bible and then he begins reading from another book. I suppose it is the one called "Appeal for Progress."

"This is a manuscript presented to me by a member of our congregation. I will read to you an excerpt from it, since it is pertinent to us today. If women were allowed to preach then perhaps this creative and spiritual woman would preach to us today:

"UNDERSTANDING OF ONESELF"

One's likeness, one's nationality, we know, we who believe, that we are made in the Image of God. Made in his likeness . . .

Giving us eyes to see with. But what do we see with our eyes? Wonderful, good things, beautiful things, the best things in life, the free things of life that indicate Freedom and Satisfaction. Or do we see evil, poverty, hate, idolatry, selfishness, misery, spitefulness, vanity, etc.? Behold! He made our eyes as a symbol of open-mindedness to behold the goodness of the free world. Yet we became blind. We must use our eyes for the purpose God made for. . . .

He gave us a mouth, to taste the fruits of the earth, the splendor and deliciousness of Nature. To absorb the wonderful gifts of life. Substances to nourish our bodies, to keep us alive that we perish not. That makes us strong in wonderment. Our mouths He made to sing forth praises of glory to the Almighty, and songs of merriment, for God-given life. To sing for joy, to the splendor of the earth. To sing for joy to our loved ones. And most of all for being alive. Our mouths also were made to utter words of prayer, of Love, of Endearment, used also for association and friendship, communication with each other and with God. Oh! The wonder of being made in the Image of God. Freedom of Speech he gave us. Is our speech good, for the betterment of mankind? . . . Using our mouths for God's great purposes . . . Can we breathe a word of praise to God and say, "Behold my fellowman, also made in the Image of God"?

He reads more from the text, then I hear him say, "Freedom and Justice for all. It is written, Amen and amen. So let it be, So let it be."

Then he reads a poem, I assume, still from the text:

"GOD'S ONES"

If I am a brown man, I'm delighted to know, I
Carry the Image of God, wherever I go
Or a white man, to indicate,
I am part of God, for my mate,

Or a yellow man I do my part,
To share, the face of God, his art;
Or a red man, I sense it too,
Am Godly adorned, with color true,
Or a black man, my score is run,
For I am chosen, among God's ones,
God's ones, the colors that are true,
The ones that make up the Universe,
That in his image, I am made
And I for freedom thirst

Then he says or reads:

"And God is Supreme. . . . Freedom is peace and peace is Love and Love is the
Blessed Word, and the Blessed Word is God. And the Word is the beginning,
and God is the beginning. . . ."

Then they sing some spirituals, and he begins to read the Word of God about faith, as "the substance of things hoped for, the evidence of things not seen."

"It lives within me," he says. "And is in me. 'If you have,'" I quote, "'As much faith as a grain of mustard seed, and, believe that you can remove mountains, it will be granted as believed.' God's word." Then again he is reading from the text in manuscript:

This progress I speak of is as a mountain that stands high and mighty, yet it
is my faith that it can be moved. It is my faith, and it is truth, because it is
simply the Word of God. Amen and amen.

*   I am not a preacher. Maybe I sound like one, but I am a Child of God,*
with Wisdom and Understanding, given me by God to know many things of
God, and the earth and Man. I carry the Image of God and it alone doth
reverence me. . . .

*   I appeal for your cooperation in the matter of Progress and Advance-*
ment. . . . Centuries have passed since the first promise of Salvation. . . .

If you are inspired by my text, it is well, for God has inspired me to write this, hoping that it brings about an effect of Love, upon Human life, and conduct. . . .

I predict a future Liberation, with Equality, being inspired by God who will redeem and bring forth. . . . This will be. . . . And with this knowledge . . .

I say to all concerned, let it be done, willingly without hurt or harm. It will be: It is God's Divine Plan. But will it be done with violence, fury, hurts, killings, destructions, by Battle? It does not have to be. It can be done with Love and Prayer. . . . Love is the greatest weapon. There has been an expansion of time between the attempt of freedom from slavery. But it is not justly abolished in the hearts of man. . . .

Now is the time for a Redemptive Force to occur. . . . Liberation Now!

I speak to you as a Mother would speak to her Children. Here I authorize to do so; for I speak truth and truth is authority. Truth rings for Freedom.

I speak to the people as a friend; as a friend would share Wisdom and faith with her neighbor. So will I extend my Wisdom and faith to you.

I repeat, my representation consists of Nations, not just one Nation, for within my body flows the blood of more than one Nation. I offer my body as a Symbol of Peace. I guarantee myself to Love all Nations, regardless of color or creed. I have the God-given privilege to do so. I love all. . . . And I, Woman, that I am, Represent Nations in God's trust, therefore I have the Love for Nations. God willing that there may be others to love, such as I, God willing that I may never change.

Then he reads another poem from what he refers to as a Spiritual Text:

"MY BLOOD IS FOR THEE TO WHOM I LOVE"
My Blood is for Thee, to Whom I love,
God grant me this love to continue
God grant me the privilege to pray
For Mankind good and true
God grant that others may like me be,
With truth within their hearts,
With Loving Kindness for everyone,

And peace, with prayer, may start
God bless the blood that flows
Through my veins
That cry out to Thee, in appeal for peace,
God bless the Loving soul within me,
That freedom worldwide may release
My Blood is for Thee to Whom I love;
Peace, Peace, it cries for still;
God Bless the Blood that flows for Thee,
And grant Thee, my appeal.
The land of America is supposed to be a free land, that is truth, and truth rings
    for freedom. . . . Only God could give me the Love that I have, only God
    can give it to Thee.

Again, I'm not sure if he's speaking himself or reading from the text as he calls forth for a revival:

Purify the heart, wash it with the water of life. The living water where with
shall it be washed. Let God wash the heart clean. Join in fellowship with God.
Be purified in His Love. And the Love for God means Love for Humanity. . . .
Advance with Truth, and Truth rings for Freedom. . . .

He reads yet another poem from the woman's text, since he says again that, although she's a Sunday school teacher, she is not permitted to preach. He says perhaps someday there would be no more restriction against women preachers:

"THE TOAST GOD MADE TO MAN"
I strung the lights of different
Colors higher, higher, into the air.
I drank a toast to those above me
Not knowing the time, only feeling it near,
I let the lights be a symbol of Mankind,
Each color, each light, God's plan,
An extension cord, extended to man.

I served, I worked, right hard beneath it,
Doing for each one at hand.
It was a wonderful garden party. But in my heart it was for man.
A storm approached to end the party,
And on to shelter the folks all ran.
The lights stood still, representing a storm of life, that rained
And rained on man.
My arms extended toward the sky
I wondered, then and there, just why
That it had stormed with fun in session, God's in his work, be still my mind
At last myself all soaked till skin deep, looking the thing the cats dragged in
Looked at the lights with raindrops on them,
And saw the Toast God Made to Man
That I and God had made a toast with symbol of the lights of man from coast
   to coast
It seemed God said, "I'll let you make the way for them, who are at stake
For them you alone have loved the most
And since you them Love from the heart
Then you, my child may be the start.
The start to make them all to know,
That I am maker of them all.
That I, creator of the Universe,
Am able to lift up man
And restore to him Lost Paradise. . . .

"Now that you have heard one of the mothers of the church, I will speak to you as one of the fathers of the church." He talks again about being a soldier in the last war, and that when the other colored soldiers had learned that he was also a preacher, they had come to him as if he were a chaplain, although he was not an official chaplain. He talks about being stationed with a segregated division of the army in Bristol, England, and that after the war he had been stationed in occupied Germany, working with the others to bring democracy to the Germans and to fight against their racist and racialized ideas of the previous decade. He repeats that colored people had to fight on two fronts. And then he quotes a 1943 war poem by Langston

Hughes entitled "From Beaumont to Detroit." In the poem, Langston
Hughes wrote about blacks before Jim Crow, before Hitler "rose to power"
and still being jim-crowed afterward—"right now this very hour." He talks
about civil rights activists and that he had his own "prophecy" that someday
there would be no more "appeals" . . .

He speaks of other experiences in the "Jim Crow army" before, during,
and after the war. Then he talks about a mechanic he'd met from Tuskegee
who'd worked on their trainer planes, who inspected and worked on the
engines. I'd heard about the pilots but hadn't heard of or given much thought
to the mechanics. I imagine myself a mechanic working on airplane engines.
He doesn't sound like any preachers that I ever knew.

"Freedom abroad and freedom at home!" I hear him say, and then the
choir sings other spiritual songs. They sing "Go Down Moses," "Didn't My
Lord Deliver Daniel," "Deep River," and "Every Time I Feel the Spirit."

"Ev'ry time I feel the Spirit / Moving in my heart I will pray."

The preacher sings along with the congregation and the choir. Then he
introduces some spirituals written by the same mother of the church who
wrote the appeal and everyone including the preacher sings:

"Lead me, Jesus, lead me, till my time no more shall be," and several
other hymns.

"Can I give you a lift home?" the Reverend inquires, as I'm still standing
outside.

"No, Reverend, I don't live too far from here. It's walking distance."

"Well, if it's walking distance, your soul ought to bring you here more
often. Just be careful he don't bring you while you're sleeping."

I must have fallen asleep. But how could I have been sleeping and still
heard the preacher and the mother of the church's text and all her spirituals? How could I have heard them in my dreams? I rise up off the concrete
steps. I light a Philip Morris cigarette and wonder if the Unicorn Woman
came while I was sleeping. After the preaching and singing—had I really
heard it in my dreams?—I'd dreamt about the war and of seeing my first
all-black female battalion. Rows of black women marching together. They
said they were paving the way for democracy. I had seen pictures of them

in a magazine and also pictures of several of them sorting mail. The 6888th Central Postal Directory Mallory Battalion.

"The cigarette is not godly," says the Reverend.

"I know, sir."

"When you get through with that ungodliness, don't throw it in front of this church. It seems like everybody wants to drop their cigarette butts and beer cans and whiskey bottles and whatnot in front of this church. I know Philip Morris and Johnny Walker and Thunderbird better than anybody else. So when you get rid of that cigarette and you want to drop it somewhere, drop it down the road a bit."

"I will, sir."

He's still holding the Bible and the manuscript. "I'm going to publish this manuscript and works by other members of the community. Since this creative woman gave me these writings, a number of people in the community have been delivering their writings to me. I can't read them all from the pulpit, but they need to be circulated. We have creative people. . . . Maybe someday you'll bring a text. . . . Are you sure you don't want a lift?"

"No, sir. Thank you, sir."

"Your soul's talking to you. That's what brought you here. You let it talk. And listen to it."

He waves, gets in his car, and drives off. I walk down the road a bit, finish the cigarette in front of the Sunoco gas station, then toss the butt in the gutter, cross Upper Street, and head toward Third.

In my dream, I hold her.

"Be careful of my horn," she says, turning slightly. I kiss her carefully.

"Freedom abroad and freedom at home!" I hear the Reverend shout.

He's sitting on the concrete steps of the church. Instead of Upper Street, the sign reads Upper Volta.

The Reverend winks at me: "She thinks it's a predicament of the flesh when it's a predicament of the spirit," he says.

Taking my hand, the Unicorn Woman leads me down the street. We stand in front of the Sunoco station. Then we go to a nightclub called the Black and Tan Club.

After the nightclub, dining and dancing, the Unicorn Woman says, "Come on to my house."

When we get to the Unicorn Woman's house, she walks ahead of me up the walk and opens the door. It's a cottage really, like the sort you see in fairy tales, with a green roof and gingerbread-framed windows that look edible. Inside, a tastefully furnished living room with a mirror over the mantelpiece. There's African sculpture and modern-looking "kinetic sculpture." She turns toward me and, astonished, I rub her smooth forehead.

"Your horn; it's disappeared!" I exclaim.

She glances at herself in the mirror. I see her own astonishment.

When I kiss her forehead, the horn sprouts again. "Is that the secret?" I ask.

"Blanche is real down-to-earth," Grange is saying as we work on our tractors. "She's not one of those highfalutin schoolteachers. Charlotte, my wife and her cousin, doesn't believe in that. She doesn't think Blanche needs to be down-to-earth on our level, but that we should rise to her level, that we ought to climb up to Blanche's level. She believes in upward mobility. But, like I said, Blanche teaches everywhere she goes. She teaches anybody and everybody, anywhere and everywhere. At least those that want to be taught. Not just in the classroom. And she expresses things in language that you can understand, not some esoteric language and gobbledygook. And when she teaches you something, she can even make you believe that you already know it."

"Come see the Butterfly Woman."

I'm tempted to enter and see the new woman, but somehow feel it would be disloyal to the Unicorn Woman, a betrayal.

"The most royal woman you've ever seen. The most divine. Imagine the wings of a butterfly, imagine. Wings like flowers. The most beauty you've ever seen."

His voice begins in a sandpaper whisper, then gradually amplifies, growing mellifluous.

I stand chewing salted and buttered golden corn on the cob and listen. Other men pay their dimes and enter. And suppose I enter and discover that the Unicorn Woman is no longer the measure for other women and must herself be measured by the Butterfly Woman? Suppose I discovered yet another gauge for . . . what?

"Come on in," urges the man.

A little boy pulls on my sleeve. "You got a dime, mister? I want to go see the Butterfly Woman. See what the ruse is."

He's a red-headed, vagabond boy with freckles, bare feet, and a straw stuck in his teeth. He reminds me of the little boys I've seen illustrated in the storybooks. A Tom Sawyer or a Huckleberry Finn. I hand him a dime. He pays and enters. I stand impatiently outside the tent, chewing corn and waiting for the little boy to reemerge so I can question him.

"Were the wings real?" I ask immediately.

He shrugs. "They looked to be just like butterfly wings, a red admiral or a monarch butterfly, or maybe even a glasswing butterfly or a viceroy, one of those most colorful type butterfly's wings, but I don't think they were real. I think they use projectors or something, like in a movie house. They didn't let you get close enough to determine if they were real. And some of the folks didn't want me in there, because they said it wasn't a butterfly woman for kids, but I stayed there anyway, because I paid a dime like everybody else and I had a right to be there. I bet if I put my hands through her wings there'd be nothing but air, like movies projected on a screen.

"Anyway, thanks for the dime, mister. I think it's just worth a nickel though."

I let the corncob drop and scrape kernels from my teeth. I pay a dime and go see the crocodile woman, who displays what looks like crocodile skin on her back and shoulders. She wears a leopard-skin, strapless, shapeless bathing suit and keeps her back to the audience or sometimes turns in profile. There's a bearded lady and a turtle woman, and an assortment of other female oddities, but no unicorn woman this time. I return to the tent that shelters the butterfly woman and listen to the spiel:

have you ever seen a butterfly emerge from its cocoon wings so fragile you try to get born and try not to break or shred your wings that's why we don't let you

touch her wings her wings are so delicate if we let you touch them she wouldn't
have any but every color under the rainbow and beyond the rainbow every color
of every beautiful colorful butterfly you'll see in her wings most beauteous sight
you've ever seen and most beautiful woman and she'll fly a little bit for you too
just a little bit wings like that are meant to lift butterflies not women come
and see the butterfly woman the most royal and beautiful woman you've ever
seen and the most divine I have seen butterflies all over the world and I'll tell
you this is the most beautiful one because she combines the beauty of them all
imagine the wings of a butterfly imagine wings like flowers imagine the most
beauty you've seen in one place imagine just cost you a dime you don't have to
imagine have you ever seen a butterfly . . .

I go buy another corn on the cob and return to listen. Over the doorway
of the tent hangs a medallion. You'd expect it to be wings, but it isn't. It's
one of those lion guardants that seem geared to frighten at the same time
that the barker's words entice. I wonder why it's not a guardant butterfly.
The barker pauses a moment, looks as if he's composing his thoughts. His
brow looks like half-formed thoughts, then he gives me a bold stare.

we have a gent out there who can't make up his mind whether to come in
here and see the butterfly woman or not now isn't that something I say that's
something just cost you a dime any man ought to spare a dime for beauty for
the most beauty he's seen in the world

A crowd of men circle him and spare a dime. I wonder if he'll keep that
new line in his recitation, since it seems to inspire even more men to enter.
I don't stay to listen. I ride the Ferris wheel, talk a little to the man who
tests the Ferris wheel before they let folks ride it, listen to another fellow
telling folks to come and ride.

if I don't ride it, you don't ride it if you ride one of our wheels you can bet
that Harry Merlan rode it first that's your security that I rode it first all I need
to do is listen and I can tell if a pin is loose and where they will tell you that
I've got the best hearing and have developed a strong tactile sense I can tell by
the way a wheel rides it's tactile sense and it's good hearing and it's equilibrium

I rise and fall and she makes love to me in whispers. Currents of sea, then a
whirlpool. "Purify your motives," she says. There's the sound of water in the

distance, water rushing over rock, some hidden spring. I move like a dancer. We're two dancers suspended in time. "You're a romantic," she says. "I didn't know you were so romantic." Timeless movement, now and always, now, here, now, always.

"Maybe it's only a shell, a husk, without purpose?" she says. "I once saw an Oriental woman with a horn like a unicorn's. Someone took a photograph of her and put it in a book. Do you think that's why I grew this horn? The power of suggestion? But I already had my horn."

Now we're riding together in a narrow canoe, the clatter and chatter of oars on water. Her earrings are oyster shells. Her long fingers are holding the oars. I stare at her inviolable horn.

"Those crickets' voices sound almost human, don't they?" she inquires. "They sound almost human, don't they? Almost like human voices."

I hear the choir behind us singing the spiritual "Deep River." Then I hear them singing "Roll, Jordan, Roll." Trees, with metal leaves. Desire, the roots. The sun, copper, green, and orange. Dolphins play around us. I smoke a cigarette.

"Do you think I'd be as beautiful without my horn?" she asks. The water looks like metal.

"It's just a horn, Buddy," she says, her long fingers making ripples in the water. She looks as if she's exercising her fingers. "Do you think I'm the wisest or the wickedest woman in the world? Do you think I'm divine?"

I scrutinize her but don't answer. She makes strings of her hair, to fiddle with.

The wind from the window blows over my forehead and I wake up. I hear voices from the apartment next door.

"I thought you'd deserted me."

"I couldn't half desert you."

I imagine him undressing, standing in shirtsleeves, then undershirt, then opening a window to catch some breeze.

"Come and cuddle," she says. He goes to her, or so I imagine.

BOOK II

———•◆•———

*What's in a horn? Or "Are you sure
this legend is the real one?"*

I HAVE A "SOMETIMES" GIRLFRIEND NAMED ESTA. A word about her
name. She was born at Eastertime and her parents intended to name
her Easter, but the parent who wrote her name down couldn't spell Easter
and spelled it the way he pronounced it and wrote down "Esta." However,
most people who hear the name Esta think her name is really Ester, Estelle,
or Estella. Therefore she has five possible names: the name her parents intended and other names derived from misspellings, mispronunciations, or
misapprehensions. Most people call her by the name they think they hear.
The people who think she's really named Estelle or Estella have begun to
call her Stelle or Stella. I have always called her Esta.

Anyway, Esta and I are sitting in Frederick Douglass Park feeding squirrels when I tell her about the unicorn woman. Like I said, she's my "sometimes" girlfriend and in telling her about the unicorn woman, I'm also
explaining why I've been such an inconstant lover and why, if we were to
marry, as we'd once talked of doing, I'd be an inconstant husband.

Perhaps I'm over explaining. Had we really talked of marriage or was that
just my imagination or the point of all the fairytales I'd heard or read? But
I tell her that it would be better for her to look elsewhere and save herself
the trouble of my constant inconstancy. So that's essentially my unicorn
woman confession.

Now Esta is the sort of beauty, the sort of woman, who you're never
sure how she'll react to something, either warm and understanding or
cruel and peevish. Either a bunny rabbit or a peacock. Or how I'd imagine
those creatures would behave. She can have a temper, but she's not noisy
and quarrelsome, so sometimes you can't tell whether she's warm or cruel.

In fact, after I speak, she's silent for a moment and I watch her profile.
Finally she puts the sack of crumbs behind her on the bench, takes off her
glasses, and starts to twirl them on the edge of her index finger, making
a great display of it. Men walking in the park notice her. She's a beauty,
like I said, so I watch her. She told me once her ancestors were from either

Madagascar or New Caledonia, one of those exotic-sounding places, and she's got a head of thick, glistening, healthy hair, the kind my Aunt Maggie would envy or desire. And with her, it comes natural. And her skin is dark and glowing and beautiful. She twirls her glasses and then she perches them on her nose again. Men do make passes at girls who wear glasses.

I watch her hands nesting in her lap. Her thumbs seem smaller than normal thumbs, almost like I'm seeing them for the first time. But maybe it's the shadow of the elm tree that's foreshortened them, and when they enter the light they'll grow to normal size again. I continue to watch them but the shadows of the leaves continue to play on them, till I forget to watch. Instead I watch some of the kids playing in the park.

She looks at me suddenly. Her look is both tender and unidentifiable. "I thought it was something, Buddy," she says, "because you've just been too elsewhere. You've been too elsewhere. I figured it was something. You've been just too somewhere else. You're always polite and attentive, but you've been some other place. You're very temperamental and you've always been a freedom seeker, so that doesn't surprise or amaze me. And that unicorn woman doesn't amaze me either. I've been to carnivals, you know. And they have masculine oddities, too, you know. But I'm more drawn to you than them. And you can be an odd bird yourself."

She shrugs, and I wonder if she's already been looking elsewhere from the nonchalant way she's treating my confession.

"Well, I guess a unicorn woman is as good as any excuse."

"Any excuse?" I repeat. "She's a real woman."

"I don't doubt it," says Esta. "Like I said, I've been to traveling carnivals myself. Carnivals and circuses, too, but I'm not confused by what I see there."

I watch a horsetail plant growing near my feet. I say nothing. She makes a fan of her hand, looks civil, then lifts the bag of crumbs and starts tossing to the squirrels again. Squirrels have always seemed to me the most innocent and un-cunning of creatures. But perhaps they're the most cunning, having survived so long in the territory of men.

"Unicorn woman is as good as any other excuse," she repeats. I repeat that she's a real woman.

"I don't doubt it," she says. "Somebody told me they saw you over on Railroad Street with some woman. They just saw the back of her though.

Short-haired woman, and I don't think there was anything unicorn about her. She wasn't a carnival woman."

I chuckle. "That was my Aunt Maggie. You know Maggie."

"She didn't look like anybody's aunt according to the girl that told me, and she told me y'all was all snuggled up."

I explain to her what happened, that when we were crossing the railroad tracks, that what the friend called "snuggling" was, in fact, Aunt Maggie bumping up and into my shoulder. It only resembled snuggling.

"I'm sure Birdy McDowell knows snuggling from bumping up, because that's the little bird that told me, and Birdy's a truth teller. She does not go around telling fabulous tales. She will tell you the truth. She doesn't make up things like you do, Buddy. Y'all was snuggled."

Again I try to explain. But it's no use. Aunt Maggie is a long, slender, light-skinned woman and looks younger than her age. So I can't defend myself. Esta now bumps up and straightens.

"I remember when you were a little boy you used to tell tales about Tibet and Timbuktu, and you've never even been to those places. You are a tale teller."

I say nothing.

"Well, I was waiting for you to tell me some tale," she says matter-of-factly. "And you've told me. I knew there was something even before Birdy told me, because you've been too elsewhere. I don't need to hear any Railroad Street gossip. But it's hard to tell about you, Buddy, because we've been off and on for years, before, during, and after the war. Ever since I first saw you and your father had all that tobacco hanging in his garage."

"Yeah, he was trying to start a cigar-making factory. He was drying the tobacco."

"Yeah, I remember some talk like that. I remember folks were laughing at him and calling him out of his name. I remember you took me back in that garage and tried to kiss me. You were a fast little boy."

"Fulgencio Batista," I say.

"Say what?"

"The name they were calling him."

"Never mind that. I just remember you tried to kiss me. I didn't let you then, but I gave into you when I got older, and before you went off to war."

I say nothing. I watch a squirrel scurry up an oak with an acorn.

Another squirrel is getting the lion's share of the crumbs.

"So I guess I'm free to hunt my own unicorn," she says.

"I guess," I say.

"Not you guess; you *know*," she says. "Everybody's looking for somebody. And they ain't all unicorns. I know that for sure."

I say nothing.

She says, "You are more of a freedom seeker, though, than a unicorn seeker, Buddy Ray. I don't know whether freedom seekers are ever truly satisfied. Anyway, I promised *my* aunt that I'd help her can some turnip greens and collard greens. Plus you're just so *wild*, Buddy Ray."

I looked at her quickly. "What do you mean?"

"I don't mean you're a wild man. And even when you were a little boy you weren't as fast as you tried to be. You're a good man, Buddy Ray, but I mean you're wild about the mind. I mean you're wild in the mind. And you've got an imaginative mind. So I was expecting you to come and tell me some kinda story, some kind of tale. But I'll never understand you really. You're Greek to me. You're Greeker than the Greeks. You're more Greek than the Greeks."

I say nothing.

"But I don't blame you, Buddy Ray. I blame myself. I'm a good woman myself, and you've known me since I was a girl. And I've known you since you were a little boy. And we've been some-timing it from the very beginning of knowing each other. Now take my aunt, though. She's never been anybody's sometimes woman, not her. They married each other when they were youngsters and they still love each other to this very day and to the very core."

I return to Doc Leeds just as *Amos 'n' Andy* is concluding. I hear the voice of Kingfish but can't decipher what he's saying. Doc Leeds turns the radio off and rises, startling chickens, and saluting me first as "The Unicorn Hunter," then as "Mr. Guy."

"I thought the next time I'd see you you'd be bringing your unicorn woman to meet me, Mr. Guy."

I smile. "Not yet."

"Your stomach problem flare back up?"

"No, ma'am."

"I didn't believe it had. And try some fresh-squeezed lemon juice. What can I do for you?"

I explain to her that a tiny rash has developed on my forehead.

She peers at my forehead. "I don't see a rash." She gets closer and touches my forehead. The warmth, no, *heat*, of her fingertips startles me. I back away a bit, but she moves toward me and touches my forehead again. The tips of her fingers seem trained to examine minutiae.

"Yes, I can feel it better," she says. "Turn toward the light."

I turn toward the sun as she peeks up at me. "Hm, yeah. Just the tiniest little minuscule bump. I don't think you're allergic to that garlic oil, are you?"

"No, ma'am."

"Well, I can fix you up a mixture with lemon juice and olive oil, so it won't dry you out too much. I think that should clear it up. I only use edible ingredients, ingredients from the kitchen and my own garden and the orchard. I never use any weird or odd-sounding or -tasting stuff. Like I tell our Aunt Maggie, I'm not a mystic or a fabulous sort. I use what you can get from just about anybody's kitchen and stuff that comes from nature. I'm an herbalist and a naturopathic type of person. I don't propose to be anything else."

"Yes, my Aunt Maggie explained to me about you, and that she swears by you."

"Well, I don't want her to swear by me. Sometimes I give your Aunt Maggie a little knowledge and she doesn't know what to do with it. She says I treat her like a child, but I don't. And I just use what comes from nature and the natural world and what I can prepare on my kitchen table. I use animal products very sparingly. I am mostly plant-based in my products and medicines. And I have also studied the inventions and contributions of Dr. George Washington Carver."

"Yes, ma'am, I've heard of him. I learned about him."

"Some of my products are my own inventions and contributions, and some are derived from Dr. Carver, though I'm not as scientifically minded and am more intuitive. And I am a gardener not a doctor. Like Dr. Carver

I use sweet potatoes and peanuts and soybeans also, and I put my mixtures together. Dr. Carver is a legend to me. I didn't have the opportunity to study directly with him, but I have read his writings and abide by his quotes and sayings. I start where I am and use what I have. And sometimes like Dr. Carver I speak to the Creator and try to listen. I also talk to the plants when I've a mind to, and I'm never satisfied. I am an inquisitive person. It's from Dr. Carver's writings that I learned how to talk to a flower and how to look into the heart of a rose."

I say nothing. She's led me inside through her gold-painted door, which I'm just noticing. I take my cap off and hold it in my hand.

"I know your Aunt Maggie has told you a lot about me, but I like to speak for myself. And I let my lotions and potions speak for themselves. I don't refer to them as concoctions. I've got a peanut oil soap and a massage oil made with avocado and castor oil. I've got a natural laxative made from compounded fruits, vegetables, grains, nuts, and seeds and made into a health bar. I've got shampoos and scalp creams. I've got antiseptics made from natural resources. I make my own vinegars and have a local supplier of honey. I've got cosmetics for women and shaving soaps for men. I've got things for the natural baby."

She looks at me. "I'll give you the recipe for a tonic and list of foods that you should eat, Mr. Guy. Many of these foods I grow in my own garden. I had a garden before there was a victory garden."

She writes some information for me and hands me a piece of paper. "Thanks," I say.

"I do not peek into the invisible world, though your Aunt Maggie thinks I do. I suppose my ancestors did."

I look at her. She's one of those ageless women. Trying to guess her age is impossible. I can imagine her talking to my Aunt Maggie like you'd talk to a child. She seems the best advertisement for her products and recommendations.

She brushes her fingertips against my forehead again, then we go back on the porch and she sits back down in her wicker chair. I put my cap back on, lean against the post, and continue to watch her.

She watches me for a moment, then she looks across the road at an empty, wasteland field that says "Private Property: Keep Off."

"Of course when my product and your regimen take that rash away, I can't guarantee you that it won't come back. I was pretty certain that your stomach distress would be relieved without recurrence, though. But what you have got there on your forehead is a sympathetic symptom. Yes, sir, because of that unicorn woman and her horn on the forehead. You cannot have her, so you've got what you consider the next best thing."

She glances from me back at that private property overgrown with weeds and looking like a miniature jungle. Perhaps it's the investment property of some townspeople.

She goes on talking. "Yessir, Mr. Guy, it's sympathetic magic because you're searching for that unicorn woman who has a horn growing out of her forehead that you've developed exactly where her horn is. That's as close to her as you can get. I've seen sympathetic symptoms and sympathetic magic before. I used to get them myself until I matured. Your regimen that I've given you—the ointment, the tonic, and the change in your eating habits—will clear that rash up temporarily, but the root of the cause is that you need to resolve the situation with that unicorn woman. Did you ever talk to her?"

"I gave her a note," I say. "But I don't know if she read it. Aunt Maggie also suggested that I talk to her. You and my Aunt Maggie have given me the same good advice."

She shrugs and looks off.

"Well, I know what I've decided," she says.

"What do you mean?"

"I've decided that if you bring her to me, I won't try to talk her into removing that horn."

"Why not?"

"Because that horn is her signature. I mean it has significance. I don't know what that horn might mean and neither do you. And I don't know what might be in that horn. Maybe that horn is as special to her as her soul is. Or maybe it doesn't have any meaning at all. Maybe it's a thing of importance or maybe it's no importance at all. I don't think a soul could climb into a horn. It could be nothing but bone. But it might represent an important thing. I'm just musing. I'm talking to you like I'd talk to a tree, but I know you're not a tree; you're a human man. And good-looking too, if I do say so myself. Mag comes from handsome people."

I tip my hat to her and nod but say nothing.

"Mag says the Guys have a bit of everybody in their ancestry: Native Hawaiians, Mexicans, Irish, African slaves from Morocco."

"Yes, that's the family lore. That's the family history."

"The family history, yes. I can read everybody. I can read everybody in your features. Like I said, I don't peer into the invisible world. I see everything in your features. Except for the African slaves; Mag says that the others came here and experienced discrimination and settled amongst the black people and the black community. Your Aunt Maggie doesn't like for me to say 'black.' We are still a people of color."

"Yes, ma'am."

"That's why I personalize my products and recommendations. I don't give everybody the same regimen."

"I understand."

"I've also got some American Indian or American Native plants in my garden that Mr. Dancing helped me plant. When I met him, I told him I'd heard about his people's medicinal plants, and he helped me plant some of them in my garden, the ones that will grow here and thrive, and even a few that are not native to this region. There are also plants that we all know that the American Natives use for their own special medicinal purposes, like the blackberry, rosemary, mint, wild ginger, sage, honeysuckle, licorice root, lavender and red clover, plants that everybody knows. Mr. Dancing explained all that to me and I have integrated it into my base of knowledge. So some of my remedies are based on the American Native knowledge that I acquired from Mr. Dancing. He also explained to me some things about harvesting plants. Someone saw him working in the garden and tried to call him Danny, but he won't allow that: it's Mr. Dancing. I always call him Mr. Dancing. It is your Aunt Maggie who introduced him to me."

"Do you know his true first name?" I ask.

"I think it's Ahuli or Aholi. I'm not sure. I think his name means 'drum' or that he was born in the 'woodlands.' I only call him Mister. He didn't tell me his first name, so I won't swear by it."

I start to ask more questions.

I know that the Shawnee had settled around Lexington, and that American Natives, as she called them, had been in the Kentucky area for fourteen thousand years, but Mr. Dancing was the only American Native that I knew personally. Once I asked my father what tribe Mr. Dancing was and he just kept naming tribes: Cherokee, Shawnee, Yuchi, Chickasaw, and even Native Americans who weren't native to Kentucky: Navajo, Apache, Kiowa. I don't know why he kept naming all those tribes, as if Mr. Dancing belonged to every tribe and nation.

But she's musing again about the unicorn woman.

"She might have love hidden in her horn, for all I know. I'm shy of mysticism, like I said, but I can't believe that horn's empty or that it's just bone. Although she's connected to a carnival, she might very well be a wholesome woman."

I tip my hat to her again and stroll down the sidewalk to my car.

I pull to the side of the road. There is another car that has already pulled to the side of it and one of the passengers, a handsome young man of about twenty, is making a pallet on the roof of the automobile. He thinks better of it and takes the blanket, quilt, and feather pillow off the roof, placing them on top of a nearby dark-green picnic table.

I walk over to where he is. I can see inquisitive faces peering at me from inside the Studebaker. I can't distinguish them or count how many. The one nearest the window glass, however, looks like a Tasmanian devil. I don't like that thought—but that's my true thought.

"Howdy," says the young man. "I like to sleep in the open."

"Thought I'd camp here too if you don't mind," I say. "I didn't see any clear spots that didn't dip and bend. I don't know where to stay around here. I don't want to crowd you, though."

"Sure we don't mind. There's room here. Where you headed, mister?"

"Memphis."

"So are we."

One of the little girls is out of the car, staring at me and listening to our conversation. Her hair is braided and she keeps pushing one long plait behind her ear. She's not the Tasmanian devil, unless I misperceived her like you sometimes do at first glance, and when peering through glass, taking beauty for ugliness and vice versa. But she's a pretty little girl, the type you're certain will grow into a beautiful woman. Like I said, she keeps pushing one plait behind her ear as she watches me. I try not to watch her.

She has a dark, smooth complexion and Inuit eyes. She must be seven years old or thereabouts.

"Except Mary doesn't believe it's there, do you, sugar baby?" She pouts and holds onto her plait.

"If this man's going to Memphis, too, it's got to be there, now doesn't it? He looks like an intelligent fellow. He wouldn't be going to any place that wasn't there."

"I said when we get there it'll be there," says the little girl. "I can't believe it's there now, is all. I can't believe it's there till I'm there."

"I believe there's some little-girl logic in that, but suppose this gentleman gets there before we do? It'll have to be there, won't it? He couldn't get there if it wasn't there. We're from the deepest South, so Memphis is north to us."

She shrugs and still holds onto her plait. She gives me a bold look. I glance away from her at her older brother.

"Maybe it'll be there for *him*, but it won't be there for *me*."

"Does that make sense to you?" asks the young man.

"Sort of," I say.

"Well, Mary, you've finally met somebody you make sense to. You'd better grab him because I don't think you'll meet another one."

He chuckles. The little girl pushes her plait behind her ear again. "My real name is Filicina Marie," she says. "They just call me Mary."

"Yeah, introduce yourself properly," jokes her brother. "Because you're not going to meet anyone else who thinks you make any sense."

It's twilight. I tell them goodnight and stroll back to my car. I settle into the back seat, roll my jacket for a pillow, and get comfortable. Might as well sleep late, I tell myself, because Memphis won't be there till I get there.

When I awake the other car is gone, but there's a note pinned to my windshield in a child's handwriting: "I bet we'll put Memphis on the map before you do, Sleepyhead." I fold it and put it in the glove compartment.

I sit at the picnic table beside a clump of fern. Wind blowing fern spores at me. I brush at them and think of decades ago, as a kid one summer playing with a group of visiting mountain children who believed that if fern spores—they called them "fern seeds"—got on you, it would render you invisible. They would not play among ferns or walk in the vicinity of ferns when a high wind was blowing.

To convince them of their silliness, I'd rubbed some fern seeds on me. "Am I invisible?" I asked.

"No," they replied.

"Now?" I said.

One of the children explained that the reason I was not invisible was because I didn't care whether the fern seeds made me invisible or not; if I had *cared*, if I had not been indifferent, they'd have rendered me invisible.

Being mischievous, I took a bounding leap and deposited fern seeds on one of the little girls. She rubbed at herself too late and I watched their looks of bewilderment, then disillusionment.

It seemed strange to me that, even with their precautions, fern seeds had never by chance gotten on any of them and that they had to wait for me, a city boy, to demonstrate that fern seeds did not render you invisible. They were colored mountain folks, but they reminded me years later of the Walton clan I'd see on TV and that took place among people portraying folks of my generation, and one of the little boys reminded me of John-Boy, played by Richard Thomas. In fact, like John-Boy he kept a journal, and years later, when I was an old man searching for books by some of the Black Appalachian writers, "Afrilachians" they called themselves, a book someone had recommended to me by Crystal Wilkinson called *Blackberries, Blackberries*, I found his name listed among them for a curious and experimental work he had written. I'm sure it was the same little boy. As for then, he stepped forward and rubbed fern seeds on himself.

"Invisibility is a power," he explained. "Nothing to be afraid about. It used to be a power, something to want. That's why the old people, the people in the olden days, those old-time black mountain people, were able to take fern seeds and make themselves invisible. Then people stopped thinking it was a power, something they could use, and started thinking it was something to fear. That's why they don't have magic fern seeds anymore."

Then the other children bravely came forward and rubbed themselves with fern seeds. They giggled as they rubbed fern seeds on themselves and each other. Wearing ferns in their woolly hair, they looked like elves dancing, African elves. The little girl whom I'd brushed with fern seeds grabbed my hand and allowed me into their dance.

And once again, years later, I heard my mother telling someone about some invisible playmates I'd had one summer when I was very small and that I'd called them "mountain people." I'd tried to explain to her and she'd misinterpreted it. These were real mountain children.

I expressed my outrage.

"I remember one little mountain girl that was visiting," she insisted. "Had some kinfolks around here but I don't remember no whole tribe of them."

I don't much like sleeping in the open. But the various motels, hotels, and roadside inns around here don't allow colored people, and I don't have any acquaintances in this area to stay with. But most of y'all already know that.

Anyway, I brush fern spores from myself, smoke a cigarette, and eat part of a ham sandwich, watch a few stray birds' feathers and pinfeathers dance on the tabletop with its peeling green paint. I listen to the countryside wake up, wake up with it, then climb into my car and head for Memphis.

"You know, Memphis was originally that place in Egypt," says Grange. "When I mentioned Memphis to Blanche, she told me about that place in Egypt. Now they had some real women in those ancient days, didn't they, Bud? I'm talking about beauteous womenfolk. The likes of Cleopatra and Nefertiti and such like. And all of the goddesses, Egyptian and Greek. When you want to talk about beauteous womenfolk, talk about them. Anyway, like I was saying, Memphis ain't just Tennessee.

"Civilization grew up along the Nile, or so they say."

When he says that I think of a little girl named Civilization, looking like the braided little dark girl with Inuit eyes, growing up along the Nile, gathering reeds and ferns. Then I picture her a full-grown woman, her back to me, shoulders broad and squared, with dimpled arms, looking like the showgirls, songstresses, and dancers. Next we're riding on a dhow, sailing up the Nile, sitting together, side by side, holding hands. Of course, like I said, she's not a little girl. She's a stylish woman.

"That's nothing to sneeze at," says Grange, as he reaches for a wrench. "Of course Blanche and I disagree on the essentials again. Blanche believes that if there hadn't been the Nile, Civilization would have never grown up. Me, I believe Civilization would have found somewhere else to grow up. Something like Civilization would have grown up anyhow. Anyway, it seems to me when Civilization did grow up, it left the Nile and moved further north. I used to think it settled up around the Rhine until the war. All that uncivilized behavior amongst people I always thought the most civilized, and they are some of my own ancestors. I don't believe I know where Civilization is today. It don't stay put. Civilization moves around plenty and it can stay with any people. It is not one man's invention, or one woman's either."

He works on his tractor, doing something that makes him sound like a nutcracker; he knocks on metal.

"So now whenever anyone says Memphis, I ask them which one they mean. Memphis ain't just Tennessee. Ha. Ha. They musta thought the Mississippi River was the New Nile. 'Art for Eternity,' that's a concept Blanche says we got from the Egyptians, the idea of art as not just for now, but for always."

Memphis is not just Tennessee. Paris is not just Kentucky. I guess France never existed for me until the war and I was there. Then the war was over. I'd been in service and supply jobs. I'd been a cook, like I said. I fried my last potato, wiped my hands on my last army apron, hung up my last iron frying pan, and then I was liberated. Call that B-Day. Buddy's Day.

I wasn't among the fellows making a beeline for the States though. I wrote my folks a letter, the typical letter of a young man discovering a new world and wanting to savor it for a while. Of course, there was prejudice in Europe, all over Europe, and I saw it all around me, and up close and personal, but there wasn't the typical color line like in the States, and the world seemed newer in those days. So even battle-scarred Europe seemed more liberating and liberated than America.

I cashed in my war bonds, roamed for a while, and discovered places that seemed born anew just for me, or like with that little one, seemed to spring into existence when I entered them. Finally, I worked as a gardener and handyman in a small village outside Paris. I hadn't told Doc Leeds that

I knew a little bit about gardening and landscaping. I didn't talk to plants and trees and flowers, and I had only used the aloe plant as a medicine. There were country doctors and folk doctors in the little villages who would sometimes harvest wild and tame plants for medicines and even would sell them in the local pharmacies. The garden I worked in was walled in and so was the house. I'd read somewhere that it was the Moorish influence that so many of these villagers had walled-in houses and gardens. I lived with a woman and her young daughter. Or rather worked for them and lived in the gardener's cabin. With the English she knew and the French I knew, we were able to communicate. I suspected that she knew more English than I knew French but was too proud to speak it. I found this with a lot of Europeans. They knew English, but because of their national pride they preferred to speak their own languages.

When I told the French woman that there were many Parises in the United States, she thought I was joking. Well, I only knew two of them: Paris, Kentucky, and Paris, Texas. Years later, they would make a movie about the latter. I'd heard the movie was more popular in Europe than in the States. Movies about American misfits and marginal types generally are not as popular in the States as the heroic types.

Anyway, this village woman was a beauty, but she was sort of a village pariah, not because of me but because she'd had a love affair with a German soldier during the Occupation, and the daughter, it was rumored, was the fruit of that union. I don't know the whole story, just bits and pieces of it. And it was one of those paradoxes. Although she was a pariah, the men of the village had built the house for her, and the women of the village had planted the garden. She tried to explain some of her story to me.

What I could piece together goes this way:

"Je ne crois pas que je sois une mauvaise femme; je ne suis pas mauvaise. Ma beauté m'a aidé à traverser la guerre et je l'ai laissé faire. J'ai été surpris par cela."

"I don't think I'm a bad woman; I'm not bad. My beauty helped me get through the war and I let it. I was surprised by it."

Like I said, she's a beauty, but she's nonchalant about it, like a rose would be talking, without conceit. I don't know if she meant she was surprised by her beauty or surprised that it had helped her.

She explained that she was surprised that one could be saved by beauty. Surprised that she was considered beautiful. Yes, she meant that both surprised her. Her beauty and the fact that it had aided her during the war.

The little girl sat on the porch playing with dolls, the real doll her mother had bought for her and the imaginary dolls in her head.

"J'achète ses poupées et elle joue avec ceux dans sa tête." Sometimes she would sit on the porch reading her favorite poet, Guillaume Apollinaire, while I worked in the garden. She said I was free to borrow books from her library, although they were mostly in French and German. Only Ernest Hemingway and Gertrude Stein were in English.

Once I was weeding the garden and she started talking to me about Cognac. At first I thought she meant the drink, but she meant the place.

"They've got a prison at Cognac," she explained. "Somebody told them I'd been a collaborator during the war and they took me up to Cognac. They took a lot of folks up there after the war, suspects, you know, anybody that was whispered about. They had a dossier on me. It was just a small dossier. They had big dossiers on some people, thick as your fist, but they had only a small one on me. I was three weeks up there. They put my little girl in there with me. They didn't know what else to do with her. The strange thing is they never brought me to judgment. I kept waiting for them to judge me and they never did. They sent me back here. Then the people came and built us this house. That's strange too. The men built the house and the women planted the garden. Before the war, plenty of men wanted me. I'm still pretty, but no one treats me like an object of desire anymore. But they buy my flowers. I set up my stand outside the wall and they buy flowers from me, the men and the women both."

I said nothing. I pulled up weeds from the base of a rosebush. I looked at her from the corners of my eyes.

"It was such a tiny dossier. What can you say about a woman in love? My name's bigger than my dossier."

Her name is Avia-Marie Bonbecasse.

"Que dire d'une femme amoureuse? It's all so strange," she continued. "It's strange how the world can turn upside down and never right itself, or never seem to. Maybe for some people it's right side up, but not for me." She shrugged. "Before the war, I used to spend summers in Berlin. When I was a little girl, I had all the German friends in the world. All the German friends you can imagine. And there was this special little boy. That's the one they say I collaborated with. I knew him before the war. I knew him when he was a little boy and we played together. We were fast friends. I knew him during the glory days before anyone knew there'd be another world. We weren't supposed to recognize each other, but how could we not? How could he not stay special for me?"

She looked at me intensely. I was still looking at her from the corners of my eyes as I pulled up weeds. She gave his name. Gunter? Herman? Josef? Oskar? Ernst?

"You couldn't invent a better world than the way Berlin used to be in the old days. You couldn't invent a better world than that. Sie konnten nicht eine bessere Welt erfinden als das. I had a right to recognize him.

"We were such fast friends when we were children. Of course I couldn't imagine setting foot in Berlin today. But when I was a child, you couldn't have invented a world any better. We had tea parties. We went to the beach. The Germans were very romantic. You wouldn't think so. Aber sie waren sehr romantisch. Sie hatten das romantischste Feingefühl."

She spoke German with ease, as if she thought I understood her. I barely understood her French.

She was silent, then she said, "The air was soft and warm. He wrote me a letter asking me to come, but I couldn't set foot in Berlin today. The world was soft and warm then."

That night she came to my room. She picked at her hair till it stood up like a kingfisher's.

"Sind Sie einsam?" she asked me, as if we were both in Germany, not in France. "Are you lonely?"

We became lovers. She had tea parties for me and we found beaches and brought the little girl along, playing with her dolls, visible and invisible ones. We went to a local farm and watched the ostriches do their traditional springtime dance. Avia, in a fit of laughter, joined them. She danced in the shadow of the great birds, flapping the lovely skirt of her summer dress. One of the ostriches was smaller than the others and looked more like it was being chased than dancing. It had three toes instead of two, but its feathers were more colorful than those of the other birds, and I wondered if that was what counted for a bird, the colorful feathers. When the farmer returned the strutting ostriches to the barn, Avia danced with me. The farmer eyed us, not with distrust but curiosity.

"He wouldn't dance with the birds either. We did this when he was here, mon ami allemand. I brought him to this farm so that he could watch the ostriches do their springtime dance. He thought it was the silliest thing he'd ever seen, me dancing with these birds."

She flapped her dress again. It was made of some soft, sheer, yellow fabric that looked like pina cloth. She wore a necklace of green glass.

"We did this when he was here. He thought it was the silliest thing he'd ever seen," she repeated, as if she'd forgotten she'd told me, or needed to repeat it for the benefit of her own memory of revelation. "But sometimes you need to be silly, even during a war. Peut-être précisément en temps de guerre."

"Why does our duck waddle?" asked the little girl. She stopped for a moment playing with her dolls and watched the duck.

We had returned to find her playing near the garden's small pond, a neighborhood woman watching her. I'd asked Avia why she hadn't taken the girl along to dance with the ostriches and she'd said that they frightened the child: "She thinks birds aren't supposed to be bigger than she is."

"Because all ducks waddle," explained Avia. "A duck waddles. Tous les canards se dandiner."

"If I were a duck I wouldn't waddle. Je ne me dandinerais pas si j'étais un canard."

"You would. All ducks waddle. You'd have to. All ducks do. If you were a duck, you'd waddle right along with the other ducks."

"No, I wouldn't," insisted the little girl. "If I were a duck I'd teach myself not to waddle. I'd study the way human beings walk. I'd be the only duck to move like a human being."

"After the war he wrote me the most delicate letter asking me to come. It was a love letter, but it was a letter of disillusionment too. He said we were all victims of our times, all pigeons. But even the pigeons weren't innocent, he said. Sogar die Tauben waren nicht unschuldig. A strange thing to put in a love letter. But

he expressed everything so delicately. It was the most delicate, gentlest letter I've ever received. It wasn't a very long letter either but it had everything a man could say to a woman. Il semblait trop délicat pour avoir été soldat."

Then one morning there was a note slipped under my door. Scribbled on the edge of what resembled wallpaper, it told me to please go. As an explanation it gave: "I can't go back to Cognac." I packed my bags and left. I often wonder how long I would have stayed. Sometimes when I think about her today, she doesn't seem real to me. She seems the sort of woman one reads about in books or sees in movies. Once I dreamt of her, stepping back into the pages of a book. Another time she descended from a movie screen.

I left for the little village that was the French term for "Crow's Nest" and there I met a woman who had served in the French Resistance. Unlike with Avia, people treated her like a heroine. They treated her with great respect. She had been part of a resistance network. We were not lovers.

I'd heard about a lecture she was giving about French women in the Resistance and the Resistance networks during the war and so went to hear her speak. I had learned enough French by then to understand most of what she was saying. She talked not just about French women who fought for a free France but of the efforts of women in the occupied USSR, in Yugoslavia, in Greece, in Italy. She explained that she was working on two books simultaneously, "Women and the French Resistance" and "Women and Freedom Movements." I was one of the few men sitting in the audience, and so she came up and talked to me afterwards. In fact, she made a beeline straight for me.

I said, "Hello."

She said, "Oh, you're an American. I thought you were Algerian. You're one of the liberators. Most men don't like to hear women talk about war and politics. But you must be different."

"You had to see some action," she's saying. "I don't believe you could go over there without seeing *some* action."

I touch her jawline. I assure her that I did see some action.

"I know you did, Buddy. You couldn't go to a whole war and not."

We're upstairs in the boardinghouse where she's staying. It's called Wooley Boatman's after the woman who owns it. Now that's a name to have and a name to remember.

"Wooley, this is my cousin Buddy from Kentucky. He's going to be staying with me for a few days. He used to be a soldier." Actually she says, "He's a farmer soldier."

Wooley looks at me like she hardly believes I'm the young woman's cousin and if I used to be a soldier in the recent war, even a "farmer" one, I was the boogie-woogie bugle boy.

"None of my business," she says, and gives the young woman an extra key.

And I should say that Wooley looks like her name. She's a middle-aged black woman with woolly gray hair. And it looks like an Afro before the days when Afros were in vogue. I must have been looking at her like she was a wild woolly mammoth, because she gave me the same regard.

And you have to remember her, the young woman who liked the fog, who got all romantic in it, who wished she could have been somebody's dear (not deer) during the war. I've driven back to Memphis to see her. I carry my bag up to her room.

She's got a cot in the room along with her bed. She glances at me shyly. I realize just how young she is. She's not underage, but she's still a young woman. Young to me.

"I had to borrow the cot, so that Wooley would better believe me, but she knows you're not my cousin, unless it's *kissing*."

Remember "kissing cousins"? I don't know if people still use that expression in this new day and age. "This is my kissing cousin," people used to say in the old days. I believe it meant you were distant enough to kiss without scandal.

Anyway, so I touch her jawline, and she scoots up closer to me. She's got the two biggest pillows that you've ever seen and we're both perched against one. I'm wishing her name was Wooley Boatman, but it's Gladys.

"This one soldier told me that they wouldn't even give y'all any peace during the war."

"What do you mean?" I ask.

"I know war and peace ain't the same thing," she said. "But this one soldier told me that these white soldiers were telling all the women over there that colored soldiers had tails. He said he went out with this one woman and she asked him to show her his tail."

"Did he show it to her?"

"You're awful, Buddy. That's nothing to joke about. He said she was so innocent looking when she asked him that he couldn't be mad at her.

"But these white soldiers that told that lie weren't innocent. They weren't innocent at all. They portray them as American innocents, but they're not."

"So what did he tell her?"

"He just explained to her real politely that no, colored soldiers did not have tails, and that satisfied her."

"That was enough to satisfy her?"

"Buddy, don't joke. This is a serious matter. He told me they had colored women over there overseas also. He said he was surprised at how many colored people there were over there, speaking French and German and Arabic and the King's English. And he met a lot of Africans, and the so-called innocent Americans portrayed them as having tails too. It's funny how you think there aren't any colored people anywhere else in the world until you see yourself."

She scoots closer to me. I kiss her eyelashes. We make love.

"Did you make love to any of the women over there overseas?"

"Yeah."

"But you won't go into details."

"No."

"I bet women are the same the world over," she says. "I bet we're all the same. I don't think we're as different as they portray us to be."

I say nothing.

"I don't think any of those women were better than me either," she says.

I say nothing. I lean back on one of the huge pillows.

"Buddy, you're a strange fellow."

"What do you mean?"

"You never tell me any stories about the Jim Crow Army like the other colored soldiers do. They're always telling those tales, although there are some matters about the war they won't reveal to me. Didn't anybody ever tell anybody that you had a tail?"

"Not that I heard about."

"Didn't anybody ever ask about your tail?"

"Yes, some have asked about my *tale*."

"Buddy, are you joking again? I'm being serious. But you're a curious fellow. You always hold your head up and you walk around Memphis like you own the place. I don't mean in an arrogant or conceited way, just in a natural way. Like you have natural ownership of the place. Nobody ever said you used to swing from trees? You never confide to me your wisdom."

"My grandfather, who was born in slavery time, always told me to hold my head up. And we had a Shawnee man in our community who once saw me walking around with my head held down, and he also told me to hold my head up. So I guess I just naturally started holding it up. Even when it gets me in trouble. But I didn't know I walked around like I owned Memphis or any other place."

"Yes, you sure do. You walk around like you've owned Memphis since the dawn of time. And that's the same way Miss Wooley Boatman is. She goes about like she has ownership of the town. And not in a conceited way. You both are curious people. Me, I don't own anything, except maybe myself."

"That's a lot to own."

"And you are a jokester to boot. But Miss Wooley don't joke; she don't joke about nothing."

When I told her about staying in a little village outside of Paris whose name in English meant "Crow's Nest," (though I didn't tell her all the details) she looked amused, then she said, "I guess Jim ain't the only crow. I guess there are crows that ain't named Jim. You know what a 'crow's nest' is, don't you, Buddy? That's where we're allowed to sit in the balcony of the white theatres."

"I thought that was the peanut gallery," I said.

"Well, we call it the crow's nest around here."

"Do you know the joke about the elongated spine?" Gladys asks, looking across at me. We're sitting up in bed sharing a cigarette and a half pint of gin. (I used to smoke and drink in those days.) She's one of those women who can be real close to you but sometimes look at you as if she's looking at you from a distance.

"No," I say.

"I believe it's a joke, but it might have been something that really happened. That's the way you are, Buddy. You take something that really happens and then make a joke out of it."

"Yeah?"

"Well, what happened, I mean the joke is this: This woman had a baby. It was a right healthy and pretty girl baby except there was one thing wrong with it. Now the doctor didn't want to scare the woman too much, and so he wraps the baby in a blanket and as he hands it to the woman he says, "Now So-and-So, you have got you a real nice healthy pretty girl baby except there is one thing wrong with her.' The mother takes the baby and asks, 'What is it, Doctor?' Doctor says, 'She has got a slightly elongated spine.' The mother turns the baby over and pulls the blanket aside. 'Elongated spine?' she asks. 'Looks like a tail to me.'"

I say nothing.

"So you see, Buddy, there are true human beings who have elongated spines, although they are not rightly called tails."

I start to tell her about the unicorn woman and other carnival spectacles I've seen, but instead I fall asleep.

When I wake up, Gladys is sitting up in bed looking at me.

"Look at you," says Gladys. "I bet that's the same face you had when you were a little boy. Older, but still the same face."

I glance across the room and glimpse my face in her dresser mirror but can't read it.

"I bet you could be a disagreeable little boy when you wanted to be, but always curious about everything and everyone. And I bet you were just as unknowable and secretive."

When a rooster crows, I still hear cock-a-doodle-doo. Avia hears cocorico. I wonder if I will ever hear cocorico. She enters my room and says "Coucou," a call of endearment.

"Bonjour. Vous êtes un américain? Vous êtes un des libérateurs. J'ai cru que vous étiez algériens."

I was a little boy listening to the preacher. Not the revivalist preacher.

But the one who was preaching after the first war, the one my father had fought in.

"Some of you young men don't know what freedom is," says the preacher. "You've been through the Great War and you still don't know what freedom is. We always think we'll gain our freedom if we fight in their wars. You hear talk today about angry young men, angry young men, all the angry young men. That is glamorous vocabulary. Righteous anger is the only anger that is acceptable to God. I know some of you women don't like to hear my sermon for young men. But you have got your own tales to tell."

"That is true," said one of the women in the congregation. "No truer truth was ever spoken."

"As your Shepherd, I don't want any of you to go astray."

"We're not sheep," said someone.

"That's true," repeated another. "No truer truth was ever spoken."

"You're right, Miss Delilah," said the Reverend to the old woman.

"And what about angry young women?" asked Miss Delilah, an elder of the church.

I dreamt that I was sitting in her lap and anchored in her bosom. She laughed and rubbed my hair.

"For all of us, the war continues," said the preacher, "whether we labor abroad or at home. . . . whether we fight abroad or at home. Then he read from a poem by a man named W. E. B. Du Bois about returning soldiers: "We return. We return from fighting. We return fighting."

"When they first invaded, a lot of people thought that meant the Germans had won the war," said Avia, narcissus in her hair. She worked beside me in the garden. "They thought that meant the Germans had won. A lot of people thought that, but the invasion was just the beginning of the Occupation. When they marched into Paris . . . "

She talked of what it felt like to live in occupied territory. When she talked like that, I thought of Mr. Dancing, the Shawnee. Then I kept listening to her.

"I just felt like I was living underground until the war was over, except for him, my friend from the old days. It was like living underground."

The woman who was in the French Resistance, once she learns that I am an American—she says "American," not "American Negro"—sits down beside me and talks about what it was like for the women working in the French Underground.

"Donc vous êtes un des hommes qui est venu pour entendre une femme parler de la guerre et de la politique."

She explained that it always surprised and intrigued her, the men who would come to hear a woman speak of war and politics. Certain men in the Resistance were very much against the participation of women.

"It was like living underground," Avia is saying. "I knew people, even women, in the Underground. They couldn't understand me. But they knew about Berlin in the old days."

I'm in the kitchen drinking coffee when Wooley Boatman enters. She has one of those faces that captures your attention. Her whole head of hair is white and it's not straightened, which was unusual in that time. Her face is the color of brown pancakes and slightly flushed.

"Good morning, *Cuz*," she says. She emphasizes the "Cuz" like she still doesn't believe that's my true relationship to Gladys. In fact, she knows for sure it's not.

"Good morning, Miss Boatman." I'm not wearing a hat, but I tip an imaginary hat to her. Someone once told me that gentlemen should do that and so I'm always doing that. I don't remember who I learned it from.

Perhaps my father? *Show respect for yourself and show respect for other people.* I don't remember my father ever sitting me down and having a talk with me. He just taught me by example.

"I see Gladys told you about the coffee, but if you want anything special for breakfast you have to wait for me."

And that's all she says.

She fixes a big skillet of scrambled eggs, a big skillet of bacon, a big skillet of ham, a heaping skillet of pancakes, a boiling pot of brown sugar and cinnamon syrup. She puts butter and cheese in the grits. I sip coffee and listen to things being fried and simmered. I drink my coffee black.

Gladys always loads hers with cream and sugar. Or she doesn't drink it at all.

When I asked Gladys about Miss Boatman's hairdo, she said as far as she knew the Boatman women had always worn their hair in the natural way ever since slavery days and clear back to Africa; it was not a style peculiar to Miss Boatman. It was a style that she had, in other words, inherited. And she didn't know if her true name was Wooley or if that was a nickname the people in Memphis called her because of her extraordinary hairdo or "hairdon't," some signifying people said. But years later I would see all kinds of women wearing their hair like that, even movie stars.

In the walled-in house in "Crow's Nest" one smelled nothing in the mornings— then there was bread, fresh butter, jam, milk, and chicory tea. Infusion, Avia called it.

"C'est le petit déjeuner typiquement français. Ce n'est pas comme vous les Américains."

Wooley. I stare at the back of her head. It's either a nickname or her real name, Gladys had said. She just knew that the people in Memphis had always called her that and that she called herself that. Unlike most people, she adored her name. At any rate, she'd grown into her name, Gladys had said. And the older she got, the more of a "Wooley" she had become. There seemed to be no distinguishing her from her name. I watch her stirring a pot of oatmeal and then a pot of grits. These pots, plain oatmeal and plain grits. As she's turning, I glance away from her, holding my cup of coffee with both hands. It's still steaming and too hot to hold with bare hands, but I hold it anyway.

"Well, this ought to last the morning for the hungry bunch that lives here," she says. "And keep the eggs covered so they won't dry out, will you, Mr. Buddy? These pancakes stay warm if you keep them in the warmer."

She marches out of the kitchen, her house shoes slapping her heels. I put the hot cup down and wait for Gladys before I eat breakfast.

"Wooley Boatman's kind of aloof," I say.

"Doesn't she remind you of an old woolly mammoth?" asks Gladys. "But she's a nice lady. I adore her."

We sit at one end of the long table. An old man with a beard like spun sugar sits at the other end. None of the other boarders have descended yet. The old man acknowledged us when he entered, nodding his head to us. I heard Gladys call him "Mr. Daw." He doesn't sit close to us or join us in our conversation. He chews his pancakes and it seems as if the space around him is reserved.

"Oh, yes she's real nice, a real nice lady, Miss Boatman is," says Gladys. "It's just that you're a stranger and she doesn't take to people right off. She has to know them for a while. She will have to get to know you."

I chew a piece of bacon, then wipe my greasy fingers on a crust of bread. Gladys butters her pancakes and pours on a copious amount of brown-sugar syrup. The old man gets up and pours grits into a bowl, the plain grits, not the buttery, cheesy grits, and comes back to the table.

"She used to be a nurse in the other Great War. People say that she was a nurse with the Red Cross, but when she got back from the Red Cross she wasn't allowed to do any nursing stateside, so she just set up this boardinghouse. She cooks and does laundry and cleans, but she doesn't do any nursing work. She nursed colored soldiers and prisoners of war, they say. At least that's her tale that I know about. People tell me tales about Miss Boatman, but she doesn't talk about herself. She never tells her own story. I guess she had to take to people when she was a nurse but now she runs a boardinghouse, and it's filled with all kindsa people. She doesn't like to be bossed and bothered. I know what she means."

"That's right," chimes in Mr. Daw. "And she doesn't tell her own story, no sir. You have to learn about her the roundabout way."

———————————

Upstairs, Gladys sits on the bed and pulls on her silk stockings. She puts on her uniform. She's a waitress at a nearby coffee shop.

"I don't know how long I'm going to stay here," says Gladys. "I might move."

"Why? It seems like a comfortable enough place," I say. "And you say you like the lady who runs the place."

"It is. And Wooley is great. But Wooley knows you ain't my cousin. I've got to see her every day, and I don't like the way she looks at me now. Like I'm a devil. You'd swear I had horns."

I flinch.

"You're a good woman, Gladys. Wooley knows that."

"She's from a previous day and age. She's not a modern woman. I've seen photographs of those colored women who were nurses in the Great War. I tried to spot Wooley in one of them but I didn't see her. But she isn't the type of woman to take lightly to any shenanigans."

"She was young once. She's probably had lovers. Maybe here and abroad."

I try to imagine Wooley in her younger days. A modern woman for her time. Before the war, then the Jazz Age. The Roaring Twenties.

Gladys goes to the dressing table, puts her hair up, and puts on a little lipstick and a touch of powder. She keeps glancing at me while making herself up.

"You get a bigger tip if you look nice," she says. "But that's not why I look nice. I just like to look nice. I like to look nice for myself. Not too nice. Because then you get in trouble."

I say nothing. She puts on her sweater, a long cardigan, and picks up her purse. She looks almost too nice.

"You know," she says, shrugging, "I'm just one of those people who's sensitive to other people's judgments. I'm just too sensitive. Especially the judgment of people like Wooley. I don't like Wooley to look at us like we've got horns. Like we're devils, or at least devilish. I know you're a nice guy, as nice a guy as they come. But Miss Wooley doesn't know that."

I say nothing. She suddenly hugs me with all her might. I put my arms around her.

"I like you, Buddy," she says. "I like the way you tip your hat at me every time we meet, and I like the way you walk around Memphis like you owned it from the dawn of time. You've sort of spoiled me for other fellows."

When she goes to work I sit down on the bed and turn on the radio.

Downstairs, shuffling, clanging of forks and spoons and plates. Other boarders eating. She has a batch of paperback novels in the night-table drawer: *Love's Vintage, Captain of Castile, The Tamarack Tree, Facets of Love, Tender Enemies, A Novel Romance, Manhattan Love Song, First Love, Negro Romance*. I pick up one of her romances and began to read. I won't quote any of those books. You'll have to read them for yourself.

"He thinks my one horn means I'm a devil."
"Two horns make a devil."
"Well, I don't believe one horn makes a saint."
"A half-saint?"
"Or a half-devil."

I turn from my half sleep to the voice of Kingfish on the radio: "So, Andy, as I was telling Amos . . ."

I turn off the radio and go down the hall to the bathroom. I splash water on my face. I go back to the room, grab a jacket, lock the door, and start downstairs. Wooley Boatman is coming upstairs. I nod to her and tip my hat.

"Are you leaving us, Mr. Guy?" she asks.

"No, ma'am. I'm just going for a stroll about the town."

"Do you know this town?"

"Not too well."

"Don't stray too far."

She looks as if she wants to say something else but decides not to. I go downstairs and open the storm door and go outside. I stroll only through the colored part of town. I suppose that's what she meant.

Although I've been to Memphis several times, it's still a strange city. I look for carnival posters. I see a poster for a church festival, but no carnival or circus posters. When I return Gladys is upstairs, out of her uniform and red-fox silk stockings, and curled up with one of her romance novels. It's *Negro Romance*.

"I see you found my vices," she says, looking sheepish. "But this is the first romance I've found with colored people in it, where I can picture myself. I used to think it would be nice to look like Paulette Goddard.

"Whenever I read my romances, I used to picture Paulette Goddard and not myself. But with this one I can picture myself. I could even imagine writing a book like this."

"That would be lovely," I say.

"I know it would be. I'm the romantic type. I could out-romance a lot of the people I read about in books. Leastwise, I could imagine it.

"Somebody told me a colored woman author stayed here when she was in Memphis. I can't imagine who it was, though. Miss Wooley didn't divulge who it was. I could picture myself in a book like this."

I imagine Paulette Goddard kissing Humphrey Bogart, Errol Flynn, or George Raft in the fog.

"And fog would be nice," I say. "I mean you could put that in a book."

"Are you making fun of me?" she asks.

"No. Let's go out to dinner."

"Anyplace but where I work," she says.

"Is there a nice dance club around here?"

"Don't romance me too hard," she says, laughing.

I think while I'm there staying at her boardinghouse in Memphis that I'll get to know Wooley Boatman better, learn more about her history, her true story, but the next morning when I descend to the kitchen for pre-breakfast coffee, she has already risen, prepared breakfast, and disappeared. The next few mornings I rise even earlier, but each time she's already risen. Perhaps she guessed my intentions and deliberately avoided me. Or that is my conceit. When I do learn more about her, it's still from Gladys, and not from her directly and personally.

She wants to have a respectable boardinghouse and that's why she is so fussy about the people who stay there, although I'd distinctly heard her say "None of my business" when Gladys had introduced me as her "cousin." During the Depression, Wooley had organized a food pantry in the community. She also has a lot of books by colored authors. "Ain't none of them romantic," Gladys tells me. "There aren't any Negro love stories that I would be interested to read. When I asked Miss Wooley about that, she showed me one of the books, but it seemed like more of a religious book than a love story. And the colored lady author who stayed here, I don't think she wrote romances. But the book Miss Wooley showed me was about religion."

"Oh, you must be talking about Miss Zora Neale Hurston's *Their Eyes Were Watching God*," I say. "That is indeed a love story."

"That sounds like a religion book to me, so I didn't take it when she offered it. How do you know that book?"

"My mother has a copy of it. She's a fan of Miss Hurston. She has all her books. She has works by colored women writers from way back, even before the last century. She's a collector and a fan of them. She's even found some works still in manuscript. But the book you're talking about is a love story."

"Well, tell me something. I thought it was a study of religion and to teach us how to be more religious and spiritual. I might borrow it from Miss Wooley since you say it's a love story."

I spend several days with Gladys. We stroll around some of the black neighborhoods in Memphis. She points out Melrose High School, where she went to school. And we catch a movie at the Handy Theatre, which is a colored theatre like the Lyric where I'm from, in Lexington. There's a poster advertising the appearances of Count Basie and Duke Ellington, who also made an appearance at the Lyric. Nowadays they refer to it as a "historical theatre."

Count Basie and Duke Ellington weren't there, but there was a movie with Paulette Goddard. Gladys rambled on about Paulette Goddard's shoes.

"Did you see all those strings?" she asked. "I'd like a pair of shoes with strings like that."

"Well, we'll get you some with strings like that," I said.

"They don't make shoes with strings like that around here. It takes the modern styles a while to get to Tennessee. You're just now seeing the kind of shoes that Greta Garbo wore in 1939. Romans used to wear shoes with strings like that, only without the heels. . . . I thought there was going to be a movie with all colored people, though. They said they were going to have a festival with a colored man's movies. I thought you would prefer to see that. But maybe they wouldn't allow them to show that in Tennessee."

I'm thinking of an Oscar Micheaux movie I'd seen in Harlem, that might be the one she means. That was the first movie with all blacks I'd seen, or remembered seeing. I'd even met a man who was in one of his movies but didn't realize it at the time. I'd met a man in Manhattan when I was passing through New York after the army. I saw this colored man and stopped him on the street and asked him how to get to Harlem.

"You a country boy?"

"Yes."

"Tennessee?"

"Kentucky."

"Close enough."

I told him I'd been overseas and was just getting back to the States. "Kinda late getting back from overseas, ain't you, son?"

"Thought I'd look around a bit while I was there."

"I know what you mean. I've been to Europe, but I always find my way back here. Some fellow asked me how I can love a country that doesn't love me back. But, young man, I won't just point you toward Harlem; I'll take you there myself."

We had a drink together in Harlem, at one of the clubs, but I hadn't recognized him as anybody famous until someone came up to him for his autograph. He chatted with the man a bit, then signed his name.

I'd never been with anyone famous enough for autograph seekers. I was too embarrassed or too foolish to ask him his name. When he wanted to buy me another drink, I bought him one. He seemed surprised and flattered. It was only later, sitting in a dark theatre in Harlem, watching the Oscar Micheaux movie, that I recognized the man. He was older now, but it was him.

I was still in France during tulip season. I got a temporary job at a tulip farm boxing tulips that were to be shipped all over the world. I remember what the man said who owned the farm, what he said were his reasons for growing exclusively the tulip: because they are the heartiest of flowers. And I wondered whether someone would grow something for the opposite reason: that they were the most fragile and delicate of flowers.

I'm just about to enter Gladys when she jumps up, runs across the room, grabs a sack, rushes out and down the hall to the bathroom. When she returns, she explains that her period has just started. If it were any other woman, I'd think this was some juvenile maneuver. She explains that her body always gives her a signal just before the blood starts to flow. She can't explain what the signal feels like, but she got the signal. She chats away to me.

She puts the bag back in the dresser drawer, sits down at her dressing table, and looks like she's meditating. She makes little sounds of distress, like she's cramping, then leaves the room again. When she returns she has two giant, dusty hot water bottles, borrowed from Wooley. She ties one to her stomach, the other to her lower back, then she climbs into the bed beside me. I listen to little sounds of distress and think of an anthropology book I'd once read that said that certain African tribal women didn't feel menstrual distress. I wondered what was the difference between them and Gladys and certain other women I knew. Diet? Exercise? The water? Certain herbs or plants they knew about? I remember my Aunt Maggie got a mixture of certain herbs from Doc Leeds that she made into a tea. How I learned that I don't remember. Most women did not chat to me freely about their periods. Most of what I knew I learned instinctively, or from books.

But I also remember reading that these African tribal women—what tribe I don't recall—were also shut away from their community, from their village, and especially men weren't supposed to look at them during that time. I suppose they were considered unclean. I remember reading a lot of myths and fables about women and their periods. However, I sat on the bed and watched Gladys and even touched her forehead.

She explains that the pains only last two or three hours at the very beginning of her period and then after that she feels normal. But she doesn't make love during her period, because it makes her feel uncomfortable. She knows some men don't mind making love during a woman's period, but she just feels uncomfortable. Then she gives me an odd look. She says that since she's not capable of lovemaking because of her period, that perhaps I'd want to spend my vacation elsewhere. She means perhaps with another woman, but she doesn't say so.

I grimace and tell Gladys that on the contrary I enjoy her company and wish to spend the whole of my vacation with her, period or not.

"You get more vacations than anybody I know about," she says. "You seem like a hardworking man, but you sure get a lot of vacations."

"I just call 'em vacations," I said. "It's really called getting laid off. Some months things are really hectic, you know, all the tractors in the world to repair and other times not a tractor one. So I get a vacation. Terms of my contract."

"You could travel around to the farms and repair tractors and other farm equipment. You could work on your own and be your own man."

"I prefer to stick with the farmers I know and those that know me. You never know what you'll find here and abouts. I mean, if I were an itinerant tractor repairman."

"I know what you mean. You being a colored fellow and all. They might accuse you of trespassing. You could work for colored farmers, but I don't know many of them that owns their own forty acres. I know a few that's sharecroppers and hired help. I know a man that owned his own farm and then had trouble with the deed, at least the people claimed there was a problem with the deed. Wooley says she knows a black woman that owns her own fields, but they've tried to run her off the land. Wooley took me to her farm and it's a beautiful sight to see. When slavery was abolished a lot of colored people thought they were going to get farms as a way to feed themselves and free themselves and earn money from the crops they produced. There used to be more colored farmers around here though. I know a little bit about their history. But as for you, Buddy, I thought it was something, because I thought you got more vacations than anybody I know. I thought you must be a holidaymaker or something. But I can tell you're a hardworking man because of your hands. I never much liked farm work myself, though I wouldn't mind keeping a small garden."

She sits up, her hands on the hot water bottle tied to her stomach. "If I were smarter, I'd like to be a schoolteacher," she says.

"You're pretty smart," I say.

"But not schoolteacher smart. I listen to people and learn a lot through hearsay. And there are a lot of comings and goings among boarders in this place. But I guess that is not firsthand knowledge."

I say nothing. She looks like she's meditating again. She looks radiant. I kiss her jaw.

———————

When I have my bags ready to leave, Wooley is downstairs dusting the front door. I return the extra key and say, "Thank you." Dust particles dance between us. I cough. Gladys had said she would return the key, but I had insisted on doing it myself, thinking it would give me an excuse to talk to Wooley. But she looks as if she's trying to look behind me, or under me, or somewhere over my head. She takes the key and puts it in her apron pocket.

Outside Gladys is bending down, putting spit on a run in her stockings. She rises up.

"See ya," I say, kissing her lightly.

"Sure, *Cuz*," she says. "Uh, if I do move, Buddy, do you want me to send you my new address?"

"Sure, darling," I say. "Of course I always want to know where you are."

"Of course I like it here because it makes me feel like a Global Citizen."

"What do you mean?"

"Well, when people of color come to this town and they can't stay anywhere else, they stay at Miss Wooley's. The color line is not just drawn for Negroes but for people of color from everywhere else in the world. We even had a gentleman from China and an Indian from India staying here and someone from one of the Islands. And an American Indian. Miss Wooley informed me of the fact. They weren't able to get accommodations elsewhere, so people pointed them toward this boardinghouse and toward this community."

"You don't say."

"I do say. And there was also a dark-skinned Jewish man and a dark-skinned Italian from Southern Italy and a man I thought was an Irishman, but he turned out to be a colored man from Zion's Hill, that's in your Kentucky. Some of them have come here and experienced the color line and prejudice for the first time, and others have known it for a long time in their own lands as long and longer than we have . They all find their way to Orange Mound and this boardinghouse, and they all treat it like it was a place of refuge. Miss Wooley said when she was overseas during the Great War she felt like a Global Citizen because she got to meet people of color from almost every nation in the world. The color line is not just drawn for us. So I might just stay here."

"It seems to be a good place," I say.

"It's not a fancy place, but it's a good place. And Wooley considers this community to be like Mecca. It's the oldest colored people's neighborhood in Memphis. I know that to be the truth. But sometimes Wooley tells me things I just have to trust in her to believe. But I might stay here."

"Well, let me know for sure," I say, and kiss her again lightly and descend the stairs.

I overheard them talking about me. I was a little boy. I was in my room reading a book on horses that my Aunt Maggie had given me for my birthday. When I was very young I had been fascinated by horses. Now I was more interested in trains and tractors, but Aunt Maggie still thought the horses held my interest. I sat in my room studying the parts of a horse: forelock, poll, breasts, shoulder, withers, flank, back, croup, gaskin, hoof, hock, stifle, elbow, fetlock, coronet, pastern, cannon, knee, forearm.

"He's very sensitive," Aunt Maggie was saying. "Yes, he is a sensitive boy," agreed my mother.

"But not in the way that he doesn't want to know things," said my father. "He has an inquisitive mind."

"Yes, he does want to know. He has a curious and inquisitive mind," agreed Aunt Maggie. "But he is curious about things that hold his interest."

"But he is sensitive," said my mother. "And he appreciates things.

"When you do things for him, he appreciates it. Not like some children who take things for granted. He doesn't take anything for granted."

"And he's not spoiled," said my father. "We didn't spoil the child. We don't have a spoiled little boy."

"No, he's not spoiled," agreed my mother. "But I know he's getting as woolly as a ram. He said that Frederick Douglass didn't get a haircut, and wore his hair long, so he doesn't like to get his hair cut. I don't know if that's true or not about Mr. Douglass. But ever since he started Frederick Douglass Elementary School he's wanted to resemble and emulate Mr. Douglass, who they have a picture of. I know they had barber shops in Mr. Douglass's days and times. I've seen that picture of Mr. Douglass and his hair is kinda longish, but I'm sure he had his hair cut at some times."

"That's just like a little boy," said Aunt Maggie. "Wanting to emulate somebody."

"Frederick Douglass is not just somebody."

"You know what I mean, Sam," said Aunt Maggie.

"One of his schoolteachers wrote me a note telling me that Buddy ought not to appear up to the school with his head looking like that. That we should take him to the barbershop, and even offered to pay for his haircut herself. That embarrassed me, her telling me all that, but Buddy won't let anybody cut his hair. I will discipline Buddy and tell him when he's misbehaving, but I'm not going to discipline him about his hair. His hair just keeps growing. And he acts like he's proud of his hair."

"And he just keeps growing too, don't he?" said Aunt Maggie. "Wouldn't it be funny if y'all had y'all a giant? Like those tribes back in Africa that grow so tall. They say there are people over there in Africa, one of those tribes, that don't stop growing, that grow all their lives. They don't stop growing like ordinary people. Suppose he's like that? Suppose he'll keep growing and overwhelm us?"

"Human beings are supposed to keep growing, I mean in the mind," said my father. "But I don't believe even Africans keep growing the way you mean, Maggie. And talking about them like they're not ordinary people. Our people originated from there."

"Our people originated from everywhere," said Aunt Maggie. "We have ancestors from every region of the world."

"Well, I don't know about any of that," said my mother. "But I know it embarrassed me when his schoolteacher wrote me that note about him and his hair that he lets grow so wild. I've seen a picture of Mr. Douglass, like I said. He had long hair all right, but he kept it nicely groomed."

"I have seen pictures of Mr. Douglass too," said Aunt Maggie. "And I suppose Buddy is wilder than him."

"His teacher says Buddy's a real smart little boy and wants to learn about everything and everybody, but his hair is too wild, and it makes him too visible. She says you notice his hair before you notice his inquisitive mind. Sam could cut his hair. He used to cut the colored boys' hair in the army when they didn't know what to do with it. Sam used to do a little bit of everything in the army. He worked as a stevedore and he used to drive supply trucks even to the front lines. He did a little bit of everything. He got reprimanded for protesting

segregation in the army, though. Can you imagine Sam doing all that? He said that segregation was immoral and undemocratic and un-American. And he doesn't think it was the war to end all wars. And Sam keeps this advertisement from a newspaper in the old slavery days that says 'Sound and Healthy Negroes of Both Sexes Wanted.' And a great sale of slaves posters, when they used to call us 'bucks' and 'wenches.'" Sam is like that. I don't understand why Sam likes to collect memorabilia of the old slavery days. He says we are continuing the struggles of the old slaves in this modern day and age and time, and even unto Buddy's generation and maybe even beyond that. Sam says the struggle of the old slaves continues. And when he was working on some Woodford County farm to make extra money, he pointed out to me one of the old cabins where slaves used to stay and there was straw on the floor like it was a barn and chains were still attached to the walls where they used to chain them up. I wondered why they didn't tear that old cabin down, but Sam said it was right to keep it, so we don't forget. He says the struggle of the old slaves continues into this day and time. And when Sam heard that Doc Leeds knew something about the old slaves' medicines, their herbs and non-herbal remedies, he took his notebook and went out there to talk to Doc Leeds, and you know Sam is not insistent on talking to many people."

"I know that," said Aunt Maggie.

"And Sam had aspirations of being an attorney when he was younger. But that wasn't a possibility. And can you see Sam being an attorney?"

"I didn't know that. Sam never told me that."

"There's a lot that Sam keeps to himself."

"But he jotted down the information that she gave to him, I mean Doc Leeds. Maybe that's why he makes so many dishes with yams and greens and black walnuts and black-eyed peas. There are few people he will talk to, except for me, and he don't tell me everything, and an old soldier will come and they'll have a conversation, and I don't know why he's a collector of old slavery time items. And when we drove by Cheapside in Lexington he just had to tell me that's where they used to auction off the slaves, the men and the women and the children. That was their marketplace and market center. He knows all that old history. Sometimes I don't like to hear it, but he will insist on it. And he learns about the Civil War from everybody's perspective. But as for Buddy, his teacher says he reads well and knows how to express himself and is good with arithmetic *and she doesn't have any problem with that; he has a good mind and even knows how to mind, except his wild head of hair. . . . And Sam's going to take him to the Lyric Theatre for his birthday. I told Sam to take him to the barbershop, but he's just as stubborn as Buddy."*

A fellow named Joe Pye enters and he and my father start talking about Jim Crow, and then they talk about tobacco. Joe Pye works on various farms. Tobacco farms and horse farms. And he's an old soldier, like my father, who fought in the Great War.

When Joe Pye leaves, Aunt Maggie says, "That Joe Pye is a handsome man. He's still handsome after all these years."

"Yes, he is right handsome," says my mother. "But he's a married man."

"I don't mess with married men," says Aunt Maggie. "Except one time with Petimole Cambium, but I didn't know he was married. But when that came to light I let him go."

"And then you took up with Amon Ray Smoot. Your men sure have some names. And I've just got Sam."

"What do you mean, 'just got Sam'?" asks my father.

"I mean, you have a simple name."

"But Sam's not a simple man," says Aunt Maggie. "He might have a simple name, but he's not a simple man."

"And then Dan Van Loon, from Huntertown," says my mother. The women laugh, then there's silence.

I once met a sailmaker while traveling in New England. He had a leathern chameleon face, almost the color of mine although he was of Dutch ancestry. I stood and watched him making the sail, sewing with a great steel needle. He used to be a sailor and wandering man, he said, but now, as an old man, he made sails for others to use to roam and wander.

All the traveling he did now, he said, was inside.

"I'm not like Horace Greeley," he said. "I don't advise the young men to go west. I advise them to go inside. 'Go inside, young man.' But a young man doesn't listen to that. He wants to travel out *there*." He pointed to the infinity of the ocean. "And I don't blame him, because when I was a young man that's exactly what I did myself. I ran away to sea. But at least a young man ought to do *some* of his traveling inside himself. That's where I do most all of my traveling now that I'm an old man. Too bad you can't build a sail to travel inside. But it's supposed to be difficult. Traveling inside is difficult. It's difficult to look inside yourself. That's why the young men would rather go out there, or out west like Horace Greeley advised them. And I don't blame 'em. I did that myself when I was a young man.

"And if I were still a young man I'd probably do the same thing all over again."

I stood for a long time watching him make the sail and wondering if it was an art I could learn, wondering whether they had apprentice sailmakers, wondering if one had to be a long time acquainted with the sea to make a good sail. And I was not one acquainted with the sea. Except for traveling overseas, I'd mostly resided inland. His hands were as leathern as his face. He had the sort of skin that if you live on the coast they call "sailor's skin," but if you live inland, they call it "farmer's skin."

Aunt Maggie, who was the first to see me, kept exclaiming and exclaiming and then exclaiming what a beauty I was: "He's the most beautiful boy baby I've ever seen!" she exclaimed.

My mother said that she had been thinking that herself, that I was the most beautiful baby she'd ever seen, but hadn't wanted to say so because, being my mother, it would have sounded conceited. And, being my mother, she was unsure of her own judgment. Perhaps all mothers saw their first babies as the most beautiful in the world.

"Well, he's the most beautiful boy baby I've ever seen," said Aunt Maggie, "and you can believe me, because my compliment is objective."

"There's no such thing as an objective compliment," said my father. "And you're his aunt."

"Well, be that as it may," said Aunt Maggie, "he's still the most beautiful boy baby I've ever seen. We should be proud that we've got a new bud on our family tree. And he's a smart, strong baby too. What's his name?"

"Sam wants to call him Inman, the name of some famous man."

"Inland? I've never heard of him," said Aunt Maggie.

"Inman, Inman, Inman," repeated my father.

"Sam, don't you dare name that pretty little boy Inman."

"Inman's the name of a great man."

"Whom I've never heard of," said Aunt Maggie.

"Sam knows some famous people that nobody's ever heard of. Like Perognathus Scrimshaw? You know Perognathus, don't you?"

"I want to name him Inman T. Guy. The T. stands for Tramontane," said my father.

"Not our baby," said Aunt Maggie. "You're not going to name our baby that. This is our new bud. Don't name him that. This is our new bud."

"How about Bud?" asked my father.

"What?"

"Naming him Bud."

"Did you see him smile when Sam said that?" asked Aunt Maggie.

"Yes, I saw him."

"Well," said my mother. "He recognizes his name."

"He's a ray of light," said Aunt Maggie.

"Buddy Ray Guy," said my father.

"He's a smart baby," said Aunt Maggie. "Look at him, he does know his name."

My mother repeated my name. "I like Bud," she said, "because it makes me think tree. Every time I hear Bud, I'll think tree."

"Well, it won't make everybody think tree," said my father.

When I was older, one of my schoolmates called my name and I heard my mother whisper to my father, "I still hear tree, don't you, Sam?"

Running to catch up with my schoolmate, I didn't hear my father's answer.

Once I dreamt of the sailmaker, but it wasn't the Dutchman in the dream, it was Mr. Dancing.

"I don't tell young men to go west," he said. "I tell them to travel inside."

"Are you a Shawnee?" I asked.

"No, I'm an Algonquian," he said. "And I'm a Nubian."

I remember once Mr. Dancing had come to visit my father. He sat on the porch waiting for my father and told me a story. I don't remember the full story. But this is the story as I remember it:

There was once a man in love with a very beautiful woman named Chi. He had declared his love to her, but she had rejected it. He would not eat or sleep. He would not participate in any more doings of the village.

He hoped that if he did not eat or sleep, she would become concerned for his welfare and therefore come to him, but she did not. The village, which was a nomadic village, pulled up stakes and left their location, leaving the young man, who refused to follow them. When they were gone, he threw some odds and ends in the snow and transformed them into beautiful garments. Then he heaped mounds of snow, placing layers of the garments on the snow and shaping a great mound of snow. When he had finished, he spoke to the spirit that seemed to be driving him to do what he was doing, then he waited.

Finally, there emerged from the mound of snow, scattering snow, the handsomest young man to be seen anywhere dressed in the radiant garments. He decided he would use this young man to revenge himself not only on the woman who refused to return his love for her, but also on any future young men who would desire her.

Taking the young man to the place where the village had relocated, he watched as the villagers looked at him with wonder, and he watched especially Chi as she saw him with delight and fell immediately and irredeemably in love with him.

Her father, who was chief of the village, invited the handsome young man to share a meal with them. He watched how his daughter looked at the man and saw her love for him and wanting such a man for her, he began making plans to have them betrothed, then married.

But suddenly the young man rose up, saying that he must go and that he had a very long journey to make. He left and began walking very quickly. The young woman, Chi, irredeemably in love, went after him, calling him to come back. He would not and she followed and followed, struggling to keep up with him, calling after him. He kept walking ahead of her and led her very far away and into the wilderness where the villagers would never find her and where she would never find her own way out.

She followed him, calling after him until he finally disappeared and there she was in the wilderness, calling his name, and lost forever.

Years later, I remembered reading the same story, but it was not a Shawnee story, but an Inuit story. And I also saw a version of it portrayed on television as a fable or a folktale. And I wondered at the origins of the story and whether there were African tales and fables like that.

Mr. Dancing had worked on numerous tobacco farms and in numerous tobacco factories and knew everything there was to know about tobacco. That was when my father was still thinking about starting a cigar-making business. Sometimes they'd sit on the porch and talk tobacco. But I waited for Mr. Dancing to tell me stories: about the Earthmaker and the man who healed with song. But my father would always ask tobacco questions.

"Tell me, Dan, do you believe in flue-cured, heat-cured, fire-cured, smoke-cured, or air-cured?"

Mr. Dancing felt that smoke-cured made the best tobacco. "I guess air-cured you just hang in the air," said my father. "But you've got to choose your air."

"How do you choose air?" asked my father.

I sat and listened as they talked about whether the air in Cuba really produced better cigar tobacco and why Turkish tobacco was good bong tobacco or whether it was really the tobacco or just because it was grown on distant shores.

The two men talked so rapidly sometimes it was like they were stringing unintelligible words together. The only word I heard was tobacco: tobaccowuokuchumpun tobaccokuruganijug tobaccowivantum tobaccohumguru tobaccum.

Eventually Mr. Dancing had had to stop working in tobacco because of the pesticides they put on it. The pesticides, he said, made him sick.

I sat on the porch playing with my toys while the men talked.

Sometimes I'd sit on the porch listening to the women. There was a neighbor woman named Delilah who would sometimes visit and she and my mother would sit on the porch talking.

"Your little boy is just watching me," said Delilah.

"He's like that," said my mother. "He likes to watch and listen. He's curious about people."

"So am I," said Delilah. "But I don't look at 'em thataway."

"He don't mean a thing by it but curiosity."

"Some tales aren't meant for little boys' ears," said Delilah. Then she proceeded to gossip about some "fast girl."

"I call 'em freedom-loving myself," she said. "I told her Mama not to worry about her. She's a fast girl, but she'll probably grow up to be a slow woman." She winked at me. "I was a slow girl myself."

"I wonder what fast boys grow up to be?" mused Delilah.

"Quicker men," said my father, who'd been standing in the doorway, listening too.

I drive around the colored section looking for a restaurant where I can buy some ham sandwiches, cake, and coffee to take on the road. I never like to stop at roadside cafes, even the ones that say "take-out service," which is a signal to colored people that they can stop, buy their food, and get going. Sometimes they can come in the front way; other times they have to come to the back door. You never know what the locals will do when you're traveling through these wastelands. I always keep a guide with me that my father gave me a copy of, written by people who've traveled these badlands before me, although I don't like to travel further south than Tennessee or further west than Indiana.

I also carry around books by several black writers: Sterling Brown's *Southern Road*, Zora Neale Hurston's *Their Eyes Were Watching God*, and Richard Wright's *Black Boy*.

I find a restaurant owned by colored people, go in, and have them fix me a stack of ham sandwiches and some slices of cake and a jar of coffee. While I'm waiting for my order, I sit at one of the tables and drink a Coke.

It's a between meals time of day and business is slow. I'm the only one in there until I feel a tap on my shoulder.

"Remember me?"

I turn. It's the young man of the roadside. He's with an attractive young woman. She's almost as tall as he and a darker complexion. Her forehead is narrow and her cheeks are full, so that she resembles a valentine. She wears her hair fluffed at the temples to make her forehead look broader. She wears a belted suit that shows off her narrow waist. The padding makes her shoulders broad. I can't tell if it's the style of this decade or an earlier one.

"Sure, I remember you."

"This is Grace. We just got married. That's why we were coming here, so I could get married. Childhood sweethearts, you know."

"Congratulations," I say, shaking hands with him and nodding to his wife. "Sit down and I'll buy y'all a drink."

I try to remember what he had told me before. I thought they were coming north just to get out of the Deep South. He hadn't mentioned anything about getting married.

They sit down.

"My name's Abel," he says. "I never did tell you my name, or get yours."

"I'm Buddy."

"Pleased to meet you. . . . Sugar Baby went to get you to have breakfast with us that morning when we met you on the roadside, but said you were sleeping like the bump on a log, and so she didn't want to wake you."

"Yeah? She believe in Memphis yet?"

"Yeah, she's discovered Memphis." He chuckles. "Now we're trying to convince her that New York is there. Especially Harlem, New York.

"She's read about it in the storybooks. But she doesn't believe storybooks. She has to see it for herself, with her own eyes."

"Y'all on y'all way to New York, to Harlem?"

"Yeah, Grace and I are going on ahead of the family, kind of have a little honeymoon, you know, and then everybody else is coming up there. We plan to settle up there. Everybody's dream, you know." He grins. "Grace and I'll discover New York a little bit ahead of the rest of 'em. That little girl is something else. New York ain't there till she's there. You ever been to New York City or to Harlem?"

"Passed through on my way overseas and then on my way back from the war."

"Yeah?" He nods knowingly, although he was too young to have been in the war. I suppose he's read about it in books.

"Yeah," I say.

"How could you set foot in New York City and not want to stay?" he asks. "I'm tired of these little towns. I'm too angry for a little town. How could you set foot in New York and not stay? They say Harlem's the place."

I don't answer. The waitress brings my supplies and I pay her for them and pay for our drinks. I don't want to disillusion him about New York City or Harlem, about any place really. I notice his trumpet case. I assume he's a musician, but I don't make note of it. I stand up. I start to tell him about a club up there where he might obtain work, but I still don't want to disillusion him.

"Thanks again," he says. "Glad I ran up on you again, Buddy."

"Same here, and congratulations."

"How can New York not be your dream, man?" he asks. "How can Harlem not be your dream? I can't imagine getting to New York, to Harlem, and coming back to some little town. What's your dream, man? Sugar Baby says you were sleeping like the bump on a log."

I don't tell him my dream. But it's not a city, it's a person. And that person could be anywhere. And I notice he keeps saying Harlem and New York like they're interchangeable.

I am hunting carnivals again. When I find none featuring the Unicorn Woman, I return to the tractor factory.

"Scalawag farm sent in that old tractor again," says Grange. "Between them and the Hennebelles we stay in business, don't we?"

I nod and get my tools together.

"It's your turn for the Scalawag tractor. I don't care how good a tractor fixer you are, that one's a bugger."

When I was a child, the neighbor woman Delilah accompanied us to church. The preacher gave a sermon for young people, and especially for young men. I was too young a man to fully understand him. When we came back and sat on the porch, I listened to Miss Delilah and my parents talking.

"If I were to give a sermon for young men, it would be a whole different sermon," said Delilah.

"I know," said my mother. "I know you would."

The women were preparing Sunday dinner and were sitting on the porch snapping beans.

"That's why they don't allow the women to preach," said my mother.

"Because of women like me," said Delilah.

"I wasn't going to say that," said my mother. "The Lord knows what sort of woman you are. You are better than you pretend to be."

"In the Holiness Church they allow the women to preach," said my father, who was sitting in the swing reading a book on cigar-making. But he was also listening to the women. There were leaves of dried tobacco beside him and underneath the swing where some of them had fallen.

Maybe I got my penchant for listening to women's conversations from him. Or we just happened to be in the same vicinity, and they talked so freely.

At least that's how I remembered it. Maybe if I had gone to the barbershop more often I could have heard more conversations of the men.

Anyway, I was sitting on the steps in the dancing shadow of a walnut tree. I was studying its leaves for a school project. I would have preferred to have studied a tobacco leaf, like my father, but the teacher hadn't permitted that. She said we couldn't study tobacco leaves. She said it had to specifically be a tree and something wholesome. I tried to describe the leaf of the Juglans nigra and to make a sketch of it.

"I don't believe they even allow women to preach in the Holiness Church," said Delilah.

"I believe, if I'm correct," said my father, "that in the Holiness Church they allow everybody to preach. Men and women alike. Maybe even little children. Maybe even Buddy Ray could preach in a Holiness Church."

"That's to testify," said Delilah. "In our church they will allow a woman to testify. They will allow everybody to testify. Testifying is democratic.

"But to testify and to preach are whole different matters. I'm a Baptist the same as y'all, but the Baptists are a variety of people. All Baptists don't believe the same things. And then some of the folks go to the African Methodist Episcopal Church."

"In the Quaker church everybody is allowed to preach," said my father.

"Well, it might be true for the Quakers," said Delilah. "I have heard about the Quakers and they seem like a fabulous sort of people. So it might be true about them."

"If you were a Quaker you could preach," said my father.

"I don't believe that preaching has the same meaning when anybody and everybody can do it," said Delilah. "And I don't believe even the Quakers would allow me to preach."

"But that's what democracy is," said my father. "That's what true democracy is."

"If I believed in the Quaker religion, I'd become a Quaker," said Delilah.

"The Quakers believed in you before anybody else did," I said.

"What's your little boy talking about?" asked Delilah.

"I don't know," said my mother. "He's always saying fabulous things."

"I mean the Quakers helped a lot of our people during slavery days," I explained. "And there are some of our colored people who are also Quakers."

"It's probably something he learned in a book or got from Sam," said my mother. "They're both always talking fabulous things."

"What little Sam will say," said Delilah, looking at me not my father. "Buddy's getting to be a big boy. I'm just noticing, he's getting so tall."

"They shoot up like that when they're his age," my father said.

"Don't they though," said Delilah, shaking her head.

"It's when they start to shoot down that I worry about," said my mother.

"Oh, Sam, did you hear that?" shouted Delilah. "And her talking about me. Maybe they wouldn't even let Sal preach in a Quaker church."

"I didn't mean to say that," said my mother, looking embarrassed.

"When do I get to shoot down?" I asked.

"Hush," said my mother.

"When you're in the army," said my father.

Gladys. Sometimes I think about her as I drive around looking for a carnival that has the Unicorn Woman. She's no unicorn woman, simply.

However, she's one of those nice, affectionate kinds of women. She's the sort that would do almost anything for a man, if he'd let her. There were things she would have been willing to do for me, but I wouldn't let her. The wrong man could take advantage of such a woman. You know, those loving sorts of women. I'm sure you know those sorts of women. Gladys was the loving sort of woman, but she didn't appear to be anybody's fool.

Whenever I'd go to Memphis to see her, I'd bend over backwards, though, to make sure that she realized that my feelings for her weren't any stronger than friendship or fondness or fond affection. That is, we were lovers but we weren't in love. For instance, I remember once spotting a ring, a bauble of some kind in a five-and-dime store, and thinking it would look nice on her finger—she had those long fingers, what I heard someone call "piano fingers"—and buying it impulsively, then the moment I gave it to her I realized that she might be reading some greater or stronger emotion or motive into it. She might think that I was in love with her. And that this was my "almost proposal." So I went into a long-winded explanation of how I'd spotted the ring, why I purchased it, and about her piano fingers, and that there was no profound meaning behind it. It wasn't even meant to be a friendship ring, I explained, although I truly felt that we'd be friends forever. And yes I'd actually said "forever."

There was a look of astonishment on her face, then a grimace. "Buddy, you didn't have to explain all that to me," she said. "I know it's a dime-store ring. And I know I've got nice fingers and could play the piano if I wanted to. . . . But it does make my hand look more expressive, doesn't it?" She looked admiringly at the ring on her hand.

Sometimes I would start to tell her about the traveling carnival and the Unicorn Woman, but I didn't. When I talked about our lasting friendship, she looked at me oddly, then she said, "When I do find the man of my dreams and get married, I wouldn't be able to stay your friend, Buddy. You couldn't grab me for a kiss or even dance with me. We wouldn't be able to stay friends. If you spotted me with the man of my dreams, you'd have to ignore me and shuffle along."

I was offended that she used the word "shuffle"—was that how she perceived me?—but I said nothing. I read while she polished her fingernails, mended a seam, curled her hair, while listening to the radio. I think it was a detective story or a mystery. And then there was music.

Jazz and then country. She even listened to country, and afterwards, we went out to a movie, ate popcorn, nuts, and candy, and watched Humphrey Bogart, James Cagney, Charles Laughton, or someone named Wolf J. Flywheel.

When I don't receive a letter from Gladys telling me that she's moved, I assume that she's still living at Wooley Boatman's boardinghouse. I bound up the stairs and knock at her door to encounter the face of a disgruntled old man.

"What you want, Bud, making all this racket?"

I think momentarily that this is Gladys's new lover, her "dream man," but shake that off. Still I ask, "I'm looking for Gladys Wimbleton."

"Ain't no Gladys Simpleton here. Get along, fellow."

Slam. Perhaps she's changed rooms. I bound down the stairs and knock at Wooley Boatman's door. Her head peeks out.

"Yeah, what you want?"

"Remember me?"

She gives no sign of recognition.

"I'm Gladys Wimbleton's cousin."

"Yeah, I know you. Couldn't make out your features in this light. You looked like Mr. Pollard, but I recognize your voice, though. What do you want, Mr. Guy?"

"Which room is Gladys in?"

"Ain't in none of them that I know about. She moved."

I'm silent for a minute. "Uh, did she leave a forwarding address?"

I think she'll make some remark about my cousin status, but she doesn't.

"Yes, she did, but she absolutely forbid me to give it out to anyone, not even her cousin."

I say nothing. I ask her if she knows whether that traveling carnival has come back through here.

She says she wouldn't know about that. "I don't go to them traveling carnivals myself. Not after I seen 'The African Dodger' and them making fun and games out of hitting colored people and throwing balls at them, even little colored babies, and that ain't right. They don't respect nobody. Have you seen the game called 'Hit the Nigger Baby'?"

"No, ma'am, not that I remember."

"Well, you'd remember if you had, and you wouldn't be chasing down carnivals as a pastime. One time is too many. I like the food and rides and the exotic and bizarre types of folks, the same as anybody, but that was one game too many. . . . As for Gladys, you've got to find her for yourself."

I drive around for a while hunting for carnival billboards but do not find any. I try to remember whether I'd ever seen the game that Wooley Boatman had talked about and tried to picture a poster with the image that Wooley had spoken of. Instead of that image, I see an image of Abel and his wife in a Harlem jazz club; he's playing the trumpet and she's singing. I have a week's vacation and the whole of Tennessee. Outside Nashville I spot a carnival poster: "The Biggest Traveling Carnival." Before I enter the carnival, I check to see whether other colored people are milling around. I don't want to find myself "the African Dodger."

BOOK III

—•◆•—

Are you Gamos Gandy,
by any chance?

"HAVE YOU EVER SEEN A BUTTERFLY EMERGE FROM ITS COCOON?" he asks. "Wings so fragile. It's difficult being born when you're a butterfly. Wings so fragile and delicate. You try to get born without breaking or shredding your wings. That's why we don't let you touch her wings; her wings are so delicate. You'll see her for yourself if you go inside. The most beautiful sight you've ever seen. The Butterfly Woman. And she'll fly a little bit for you too. She won't fly too close, because she can't allow her wings to brush against you ordinary human beings. And that don't mean she's shy. She'll fly just a little bit. Some of you older gentlemen might remember when we had the flying butterfly baby, but she's a grown woman now, and ready to please you. All the beauty you want to see. One of those bronze Butterfly Women. Just cost you fifteen cents. . . . Wait a minute, folks, let me tell you. There's a gentleman who's been coming here every time the season opens, and just stands out there and listens. If you enjoy me talking about the Butterfly Woman, you'll enjoy more to see the true beautiful woman for herself. As Confucius says, a picture is worth a thousand words, and the real thing's gotta be worth more than a picture. Delight yourselves gentlemen, and ladies too; come and see the beautiful Butterfly Woman."

Men crowd around him and pay their fifteen cents, and since he also invited the ladies, there are a few scattered women in their midst. I stand with a bag of popcorn and wait for the next harangue. Then, instead of paying my fifteen cents, I approach the man.

"Whatever happened to the Unicorn Woman?" I ask him.

He looks irritated and then he reaches into his pants pocket and hands me a note.

"Somebody told me if anybody ever comes asking about the Unicorn Woman to give 'em this note. You must be that somebody."

I grab for the note like it's the most beautiful thing I've ever seen. Of course I imagine it's from *her*.

"You ought to go see the Butterfly Woman," he adds. "Make you forget about unicorns. The Unicorn Woman's no match for this one. And she's younger too."

"No thanks," I say. I back away from him and open the note.

Dear Unicorn Hunter,

I don't know your name, but I always see you hovering about the Butterfly Woman's tent. I remember that you were the one so inquisitive about the Unicorn Woman. When I cleaned up her tent one evening I found a note for her, which might have been written by you. It had your name and address on it, but I discarded it, as I've been instructed to do by the boss. He likes to keep our freaks out of harm's way. Some people don't know how to behave with exotic and bizarre types of people. I've thrown away lots of notes and letters for her and can't remember all their names.

Of course, when I overheard you questioning the boss about her, I couldn't interrupt and give any indication that it was any of my business. I'm not the owner of this traveling carnival. But I take this liberty to write to you.

You are wasting your time if you come here to our carnival looking for the Unicorn Woman. She's no longer our main attraction. The boss sold the Unicorn Woman to another traveling show. I should clarify that: he sold her contract. But to my understanding it's the same thing as selling the woman, to auction her off to the highest bidder. The name of the traveling show is Wiley's Wonders. I cannot guarantee to you that you'll find it in Tennessee, since they travel to every part of the country, North, South, East, and West. I'm told they sometimes even travel overseas.

I hope this will provide you with some assistance. She's a very sweet woman, and I hope you're not the crazy type. You seem like a gentleman. The boss wanted to sell me to Wiley's Wonders, but the bidding wasn't high enough. Nobody would bid for me. Good hunting, Sir. I don't know you, but you know who I am. Sincerely,

He didn't sign his name but I know it was Mr. Masters, the little man. Or perhaps it was the boss himself, playing a trick on me?

I shove the letter into my pocket and ask the nearest colored person where I might find an inexpensive colored boardinghouse in Nashville.

"I don't know about colored boardinghouses, Mister, but we rents our attic room. And my wife makes the best fried fish and greens, and macaroni with cheese."

He writes down his address and sketches a map and gives it to me. "Just head north," he says. "It's in the northern part of Nashville. We're originally from Fort Mose, my people I mean. That's in St. Augustine, Florida, and it's considered the first free black settlement. We traces ourselves back to the 1730s, but now we're in Tennessee. It's my wife who's from Tennessee."

He seems like the sort of man who can stand all day talking about his people and his ancestry, so I thank him and tell him that I'll be around that evening, then I go and ride the Ferris wheel. I make a mental note about Fort Mose, though. When I get through riding the Ferris wheel, I get in my car and drive to North Nashville, following the map that he sketched for me.

The family I stay with while hunting the Unicorn Woman in Nashville is a family of black Quakers named Canada: Columbus Canada; his wife, Blanche; and their daughter Savegrain. Savegrain is about Mary's age and has a habit of standing watching you with her two index fingers stuck in her jaws, as if she were pointing to herself and saying, "See me." She just has a habit of standing in front of people and watching them that way.

The attic where I stay is freshly swept (you can still see the broom streaks in the rug), warm and comfortable, with a bed, a dresser, a wardrobe, and a table. Shoved to one corner of the room are musical instruments: a harp, a xylophone, and a guitar. They're not exactly these things, but that's what they resemble. And stacked in another corner is Columbus's Quaker literature, some published and some handwritten. They are spiritual and mystical types of writings, and one is a copy of a seventeenth-century Quaker petition against slavery and another a copy of a sermon addressed to "Africans." I skim the pages but don't read them.

I tell him that the black Quakers have always been of interest to me, that I used to hear about them as a child, and that it's curious that I find myself among them.

"It's not curious to me," he answers.

Columbus, whom people call "Mose," says that he carves musical instruments.

"Can't you see that for yourself?" he asks, when I question his occupation. "Some of these traveling carnivals and sideshows let me display my wares. Otherwise I do janitorial work."

He says he works at the local courthouse. I tell him that I know some Canadas in Kentucky. I don't think they're Quakers, though.

"All Canadas ain't kin, and all of them ain't Quakers," he replies, as we sit at the table eating supper. "But if ever I'm in Kentucky, I might look them up. We might be cousins."

"Or cousins of cousins," his wife observes.

The little girl loads her jaws with macaroni and cheese. They're not wearing any special outfits like the Quakers in the books.

"I know about cousins of cousins," I say, and then tell them about the first time I was in Harlem. "I met some fellow claiming not to be kin, but to be kin of kin. 'I'm the cousin of your cousin's cousin,' he said to me."

"And he probably wasn't even your people," says "Mose." (He says his wife prefers to call him "Mose" rather than Columbus.) "But the next time you're in Nashville, you know where to find the place," he adds.

The movie actor I'd met in New York had given me her name and address and said she was having a rent party, one of those old-fashioned kinds. You paid a dollar and got all the food and drinks you wanted. She was a big, beautiful, dark-skinned woman. As soon as I got in the door, she headed toward me, her eyes as bright as the lights of Broadway.

"I'm Romaine," she said. "I haven't seen you here before."

"I haven't been here before. A friend gave me your name and address and said you were having a rent party."

"Well, any friend of yours is a friend of mine," she said.

She kissed me on the cheek and told me to make myself welcome. I put my dollar in a bowl on a tiny table near the door and came in. Some people were dancing, others were sitting around card tables, others were eating. There seemed to be all kinds of African heritage people there, Africans from America, Africans from the Caribbean, Africans from Latin America, Africans from Africa, African from Europe, Africans from the island nations. They had all seemed to find their way to Harlem and to Romaine's.

There were no free chairs, so I stood at the makeshift bar made from a utility table. Romaine stood behind it serving drinks. A long banquet table at the far wall was resplendent with all sorts of foods, cuisine from the different African peoples, even Southern-style soul food.

"What'll you have?" she asked.

"Scotch and water," I said. It was New York, it was Harlem, so I thought that sounded sophisticated.

"I could've sworn you were a teetotaler," she said. She fixed my drink and set it in front of me.

"What's your name?" she asked.

"Buddy Ray Guy."

"Is that your real name?"

"Yes ma'am."

"Southern boy. Well, my name's Romaine Artesia Veronica Chandler. My folks are from the Virgin Islands, but I'm a Harlemite."

She poured herself a beer and stood sipping it. That's what I had really wanted, but I didn't want to order a beer in New York, in Harlem.

"Where south are you from?"

I told her. I watched a few jitterbuggers, then looked back at her.

She laughed.

"This apartment doesn't look big enough to crowd all these people in it, does it?" she asked.

"No, ma'am."

"Are you in Harlem to stay?"

"No, I'm just back from overseas. I went over there for the war and I, you know, stayed a while. I was passing through New York and I . . . I mean, I had to come to Harlem."

She laughed again. I listened to the music.

"Why don't you get out there and dance and have yourself a good time?" she asked. "And there's plenty of good food. Fix yourself a plate."

I fixed a plate of ham and cornbread and collard greens and stood over in a corner eating. I watched the dancers.

I noticed that although none of the men asked Romaine to dance, they treated her with a certain respectfulness and even deference, whether she was at the bar serving drinks or at the banquet table replenishing the supply of food. I *wondered how a dollar could supply all you could eat and drink, and even in those days I thought she should have charged more.*

When it was time for me to leave, I went to the bar and told her, "Thank you, Miss Romaine." I was holding my hat in my hands, or I would have tipped it.

She eyed me for a moment and then she said, "Whenever you're in Harlem, baby, you're welcome here."

She smelled like candied yams and ginger and lemon. I wanted to kiss her but didn't dare. I said, "Thanks again," then went outside and descended the long stairs.

On the train heading south, I had an extravagant and silly dream about Romaine. Romaine was Lady Romaine and I was Sir Budwick of Guy. She was dressed in an elaborate green gown and I too wore the garb of the seventeenth century, some sort of caped costume, a powdered wig, and oversized feathered hat, except I wasn't quite sure if we were truly in the seventeenth century or at a costume party. Anyway, I doffed my hat, made intricate waves of my hands in the air in courtly gestures, and bowed to her. I tried to remember what those courtly gestures were called.

"Romaine, my first love and lady . . ." I declared. She stood watching me with an imperious smile.

"That's mighty fancy headgear for a boy like you," she said. "Now what will you do to prove your love?"

I woke up as the train was crossing the Ohio River. I made my way to the back of the train.

When I returned home, I wrote a story based on the silly dream:

Having not yet found the unicorn, Sir Budwick of Guy nevertheless returns to Lady Romaine, who is clad in a gown of baptismal white lace. A magnificent feminine specimen, she is possessed of Venus of Willendorf hips.

"My Lady, I have not as yet discovered the mythical beast known as the unicorn, though I was so charged to discover it and return it without delay to your ladyship this fortnight."

"Why hast thou returned without my unicorn, Sir Budwick?"

"Because, your Ladyship, ebony ore of wonder and unsurpassed beauty, as I was travelling hither and thither, encountering and slaying dragons, wildebeests and whathaveyou, undergoing trials by water and Scotch, I began to ruminate: there I was going through trials to prove I loved you, but what were you doing to show me you loved me in return? So, there, it's out, and I attend your Ladyship's reply. . . ."

"Don't get incensed, Sir Budwick, chivalric romancer that thou art, as St. Augustine has said or will say, I can't in good conscience be loved by you without loving you back. However, being the free spirit that I am, I have loved you long and figuratively. I hope that'll do, you curious black knight, you. Or black unicorn hunter. I could undergo a few trials by water and Scotch, but I prefer beer."

"So do I. Where's the nearest pub?"

"Wait till I get my diadem, purse, cornucopia, and bric-a-brac and I'll be right with you. I only sent you out in search of the unicorn because they say that's what a ladyship is supposed to tell her knight to go hunt. So tell me, Sir, what does a unicorn look like?"

Taking Lady Romaine's arm with one hand, straightening her askew diadem with the other, Sir Budwick of Guy, being the undaunted black unicorn hunter that he is, simply looks at her and smiles.

"I didn't know there were Moorish knights and black-skinned Norman knights and their ladies in the chivalric tradition," she says over a beer. . . .

"Oh, yes, my lady, and black unicorns too."

"Let's change our names," she muses. "You'll be Guy Moor and I'll be Lady Romaine Hidalgo. . . . "

After I wrote that tale, I penned another story, not based on a dream:

GLADYS'S PERIOD

I always felt somewhat clumsy talking to women about their periods. It did not seem a proper subject. It seemed to me that women could have periods without talking about them. Still, I suppose, they had to let a man know. I suppose the word "period" itself had developed as the need for a euphemism to let a man know, or anyone else know, or euphemisms like "monthly" or "that time again." I knew a woman, though, who'd say "I'm on" when her period began and "I'm off" when her period was over; simply that, except it made her sound like a lightbulb, or radio, or some sort of machine.

I suppose having to camouflage a period too, as if it were some ob-
scenity, a side of a woman's nature to be hidden, certainly not stressed,
was a leftover or holdover from some tribal custom? Or had men invented
the words and not women? Anyway, remembering my conversations with
Gladys made me remember that time that Gladys and I were out to dinner.

(Did women feel clumsy when they told a man about their periods?)

Anyway, I'd wanted to really treat Gladys, so I'd ordered a lot of different dishes, prepared so we could sample bits of everything. I'd gone
into a Moroccan restaurant once in Paris and the table had been set that
way. I also knew that in Spain they served tapas similarly. Was that the
Moorish influence?

Instead of showing delight, Gladys just kept staring at the plates of
sumptuous dishes.

"Doesn't this look good?" I asked.

"It looks heavy," she said.

"What do you mean?"

"It just looks really heavy to me. I never eat a lot of different meats like
that. It just looks so heavy. It looks like a Thanksgiving table or an Easter
table. Some sort of celebration table."

I started to say we could celebrate our meeting each other, but that
sounded corny. When I said nothing she repeated that she never ate a lot
of different meats. She never ate like that. It was too heavy.

"I'll just have a little chicken," she said. "And some vegetables. Maybe
a piece of this fish. I generally eat light. Sometimes I just eat fruit."

"Well, why don't you just fix your plate and then nibble what you want."

"All right. But it doesn't seem right."

She fixed her plate. I thought it would be one of those scenes where
the woman protests about being a light eater. You get her to fix her plate,
and she gobbles everything and then says, "I didn't want to waste it."

Instead she ate just a little of the chicken, the fish, her vegetables, some
cornbread and some peas.

"I think it's better for you when you eat light," she said.

I finished my spareribs and then told her to pass me her plate. "I don't
want to waste it," I said.

Afterwards we had coffee and I looked around the restaurant. "This is a nice place," I said.

"Yes," she said. "It's a nice restaurant, except for that jukebox. It keeps breaking, and when it breaks it'll only play the same song. And it never breaks on a song I want to hear. But otherwise it is nice. It has a nice atmosphere."

"You're nice," I said.

She said nothing. She looked pensive.

"What are you thinking?" I asked.

"I was thinking about what we were talking about."

"What do you mean?"

"I always wonder what a man talks to another man about. I've listened to men talking to other men, but I'm there. So they might not talk about what men really talk to other men about."

"I'm sure you've overheard men talking to other men and they didn't know you're listening."

I start to tell her that I've been around women talking to each other and they knew I was listening. Maybe even they wanted me to listen. But I just listen to her.

"No, I just think men have some sort of radar and know when a woman's listening. What do you talk to men about? What do men really talk to other men about?"

I laugh.

"Why are you laughing? I'd like to know what a man talks to another man about?"

"I'd like to know what a woman talks to another woman about when the men aren't listening."

"Men know what women talk about. A lot of my books are written by men and they always have women talking to each other. Men know what women talk about because when they're in our company we go ahead and talk about what we would normally talk about anyway."

"I'll bet."

"If I were a man what would you talk to me about?"

"I could never mistake you for a man."

"But what would you talk to me about if I were?"

"The same things I talk to you about now."

"I don't believe that."

I take out a pen from my pocket and jot down on a paper napkin all the things we're talked about. I showed her.

"We've talked about all that?" she asked.

"Sure, and then some."

"It looks like a lot when you write it down. You've got 'period' on there. Now I know you don't talk to men about that."

"No."

"I bet it's the 'then some' you talk to men about. And you never talk to me about when you were in the CCC camps planting trees and doing other Civilian Conservation Corps work, and you never talk to me about the war. You never talk about things that happened in warfare."

She took the napkin and stuffed it in her purse.

BOOK IV

Getting Carnivalized

I'M THINKING ABOUT MR. DANCING'S TALE about the man who healed with song. I'm also thinking about a book I once read on Chinese philosophy that said that one could be either helped or harmed by everything you heard: I suppose they meant both words and music. I'm thinking these things as I open my mailbox to find the following letter:

Dear Unicorn Hunter,

I suppose you're wondering how I got your address, since in my last letter I said I'd thrown your note with your name and address away.

However, I discovered that I scribbled your name and address elsewhere in case there was ever any need for a unicorn hunter, as a sort of memo to myself.

Anyway, I wanted to tell you that you missed the Unicorn Woman when Wiley's Wonders was traveling through New Orleans during Mardi Gras. How do I know? Because I was there. Our boss likes to set up our traveling carnival in New Orleans also during Mardi Gras. Our exotics and bizarre folks multiply during Mardi Gras season. I know I spotted a number of unicorn women myself.

I told you she could be anywhere. I know you don't much like traveling through Dixie, even at Mardi Gras season. But at Mardi Gras everybody gets carnivalized.

Remember it's not just you who is a unicorn hunter. But I wonder what happens when butterflies meet unicorns?

Your friend & fellow unicorn hunter

"Did you like the pitcher?" he asked.

He meant picture show, movie, or moving picture.

"Not particularly," I said, chewing my popcorn. I always liked the picture show popcorn, but liked to save it till I got outside the movie and eat it on the way home.

"Why are you always using big words?" he asked.

"What big word?"

"Particularly."

"'Particularly' isn't a big word."

"You just like to show off."

"Sticks and stones may break my bones, but words will never hurt me," I recited.

"That's what you think," he said. "My mom says that broken bones heal, but words go deeper than bone."

We'd gone to the Lyric Theatre, the colored theatre, where you didn't have to sit in the "crow's nest."

I went with my Aunt Maggie to buy some doily material. When she went to the store to ask for white, she didn't just ask for white, she asked for "baptismal white."

"Give me some doily string in baptismal white please," she asked the saleswoman.

I noticed the saleswoman do a double take when Aunt Maggie said "baptismal white," then she trotted off to get the white, but she called it "ordinary white."

"Why do you always say 'baptismal white'?" I asked Aunt Maggie when we were walking down Third Street.

"So they'll give me the right white," she explained.

"I didn't know there was a wrong white," I said.

"They might give me off-white," she explained. "I don't want off-white. I want true white. Sometimes under the store lights off-white looks like true white, but it's not."

"Why baptismal?"

"Because when you get baptized you have to wear baptismal white."

"When I got baptized I wore a black robe," I said.

"You did?"

"Yes, ma'am."

"I thought you were wearing white. I was seeing black and thought I was seeing white. I know I wore white. When did they stop wearing white?"

I told her I didn't know.

"When I was a little girl and got baptized, they took you down to the river in those days. And I know I was wearing baptismal white."

"Maybe little girls wear white and little boys put on black robes," I said.

"Well, maybe that's the truth of the matter," she said.

She opened her bag and examined her doily string in the sunlight, because she wanted to make sure it was the right white.

"But I've never heard of baptismal black," she said as we walked along.

We walked along a bit until we got to the corner of Race and Third Streets.

"Pilgrim black?" she asked suddenly. "Didn't the Pilgrims used to wear black?"

I said I believed they wore black with white collars.

"I thought so," she said. "I remember in grade school at Thanksgiving we used to draw pumpkins and turkeys and Pilgrims. I thought the Pilgrims had something to do with black. But like I said, you don't need a special name to discriminate and distinguish one black from another. You always get the right black. It's that white you have to watch out for; just don't get it when it's off."

A man walking by heard her last two sentences.

"I know what you mean, sister," he said in passing.

"Oh," declared Aunt Maggie, cupping her mouth. "I always hate it when people catch only half of what you say. They think you're talking about one thing and you're talking about another. That's one of the problems of talking out in the street. Come along."

The rest of the way home she was silent.

"You're too rash," I told the little boy. "Why don't you take your time and think about what you want to do before you do it?"

I forgot what he'd done, but it was something you need to take your time about and think before you do it.

"There you go using big words again," he said.

"'Rash' is only four letters."

"It's still a big word."

"It's not a long word."

"But I sort of like it though," he said. "I thought rash only had to do with bumps. I like it when you take an old word and make it into something new."

"I didn't make it into something new. It always had different meanings."

"There you go again," he said. "I bet you don't always take your time and think."

————————

I thought my first all-colored movie had been in Harlem, but it was actually when I was a little boy. Every Sunday after church my Aunt Maggie would take me for ice cream at Tiger's Inn, which was a black-owned restaurant.

"Do you want to see an all-colored movie, Buddy?" she asked, while I was eating my ice cream.

"Yes ma'am," I said.

We slid out of the booths and walked down the street to the Lyric Theatre.

"I liked that Little Othello," said Aunt Maggie.

"But they called him Big Othello. Grande Otelo means big," I said. "Like the Rio Grande means a big river."

"It's funny, ain't it?" said Aunt Maggie. "How we're always calling little people big and big people little? Did you like it, Buddy?"

"Yes, ma'am," I said, chewing my popcorn.

"But it's funny," said Aunt Maggie, "how colored people are always calling people the opposite of what they are. I don't mean they do it all the time. But they like to do that."

I chewed my popcorn.

"Well, aren't you glad you saw that movie?"

"Yes, ma'am."

"And you're the better for it."

"So he asked me what Deli stands for and I told him Delight," our neighbor Delilah was saying.

"Hush," my mother said as I came onto the porch from school. I sat on the steps.

"Delicious?" asked Delilah, who was wearing a green, yellow, and red print dress. Her hair looked like a pile of velvet, curled and waved.

"Yes, I did bake some delicious brownies today," said my mother, trying to camouflage the conversation. "They're made with honey. I'll go in and get 'em and bring 'em out here so we can all have a nibble on 'em.

"They're light, so they won't spoil your supper."

"That's what he said," said Delilah.

My mother, thinking of nothing to camouflage that one, just waved her hands in the air and went into the house. When she came back, she held a pan of brownies and a tray of lemonade balanced on top of the pan, as Delilah said, "You ought to come over with me to Tiger's Inn on Sunday. I saw Buddy and his aunt Maggie in there eating ice cream. It's a whole different world at night though and there's dancing. You like to dance."

"I do," said my mother, putting the pan of brownies on the porch and sitting down again. I'd taken the tray of lemonade and handed her and Delilah their glasses. Delilah picked up the tray and passed brownies around, then set the tray back down on the porch. I tried to remember seeing Delilah in Tiger's Inn, but maybe I was too busy eating ice cream.

"Maybe I'll go over there if Sam wants to go," said my mother.

"You can go if Sam doesn't want to go," said Delilah.

"Uh-uh, I don't want to go to Tiger's Inn if Sam doesn't want to go."

"I saw Sam dance at Sable Terrapin's wedding. Girl, I had to laugh. He was still two-stepping. He thinks it's still ragtime, don't he?"

"I suppose he does," said my mother. "But Sam's a pretty good dancer when he wants to be."

"For ragtime," said Delilah. "But you ought to go over to Tiger's Inn some night whether Sam wants to come along or not. You're a free woman."

"No, I'm not," said my mother.

"Well, if I was married, I'd be just as free as I am now."

My mother said nothing. Delilah dunked her brownie in the lemonade.

"These are good, Sal. They taste like nectar of the gods."

"Thank you."

"Well, the night people at Tiger's Inn are different from the day people. They're a different brand of people."

"I bet they are."

"You could be a night person and a day person too," said Delilah.

"Not with Sam," said my mother.

Delilah started to say something, then she looked at me and hushed. I stretched over and got another brownie from the pan, then I went into the living room to look at my books on trains and trainmen. Their voices carried inside.

"You didn't say who he was?" said my mother. "I hope he's not a harem-collector."

"And what if he is?" asked Delilah. "No, it's Wayman. You know him, don't you?"

"Yes, I know him. He's right attractive, and he's nice too." Delilah said nothing.

"Well, it's about time you found somebody," said my mother.

"Or somebody found me," said Delilah. "And the funny part is neither one of us was looking."

Wayman. I used to think his name was Weighman. The black man who weighed the fruits and vegetables down at the grocery store where we shopped. When I first met him, I thought he was one of our kin because he looked like the Guys. He looked like our people.

"Buddy thought Mr. Wayman was one of our people," said my mother when we returned from the grocery store. "He asked me which one of our people was he?"

"He might be one of our people," my father said.

"What do you mean? He's not our kin," said my mother.

"Don't none of us know who our people are, the way we was mixed up and around and confused during slavery times. We could be related to a lot of different people that we don't know about. We don't even know which tribes we're from. I met an African during the Great War who told me what tribes I appear to be from, but I can't remember their names. We could be kin to Way and not know it."

My father called him Way.

My mother said nothing, then she said, "Anyway, Buddy thought we were kin. I took some fruits and vegetables over to be weighed, and Buddy started chatting to Mr. Wayman like he knew him from way back. Like he thought he was kinfolk."

"Who's to know," my father insisted. "We could be kin to Way."

"Well, Buddy thought he was the image of you and your people. Because he certainly doesn't resemble mine. And he's got hair like your people. Hair like yours and Buddy's. Hair like a Persian lamb's."

Miss Delilah only came to our house in the afternoons or evenings because my mother had admonished her from coming during the daytime, while she was working.

"Delilah," she said, flapping a dust rag, "I'm as busy as a bee in the daytime, and I can't talk and listen and clean at the same time. And you've got a house to clean."

"Honey, I get my house cleaned in no time. I've finished cleaning."

"Well, that's because it's just you. You don't have any men to clean up after. I've got Sam and Bud. I'd prefer you to come in the afternoons or evenings."

"I could bring something to read. I could read while you're cleaning. I could read one of my magazines. Or one of the books you've got around here. Or one of Bud's comic books. Or even the Holy Bible."

"No, Delilah."

"I'm just being selfish. Let me help you to clean up."

"No, Delilah."

"Buddy could help you clean up."

"He has his schoolwork to do. And he has his chores. He does yardwork. I don't allow Buddy to do housework. Or Sam either. I prefer to clean my house my own way. They will sometimes do the dishes. And they will empty the garbage and the trash cans."

"I'm just being selfish," Delilah repeated. "Don't you have somebody's hair to do?"

"I don't have that many customers, just you and Mag and Miss Leeds and a few others. I'll have more customers when I get my own beauty shop and don't have to go to people's houses and be what Sam calls an itinerant. But as for now my income is sufficient for me."

"Well, you're a good beautician because people say my hair always looks nice. Mag thinks someone hoodooed her hair. Because when she was a young girl she had really fine long and healthy hair and looked like an Indian princess, then when she got older it started to break off. She thinks someone was jealous and hoodooed her hair. She doesn't let many people touch her head except for you and Doc Leeds."

"Mag's got a lot of strange notions. I told her to put some castor oil on her hair to stop the breakage and she won't do it. Castor oil and olive oil. Sometimes she thinks I'm trying to hoodoo her hair. She says I have strong and healthy hair. But that's my best advertisement for doing other people's hair."

My mother said nothing, then she said, "You do have beautiful hair, Delilah."

"This house smells like walnuts," said Delilah.

"I polish with walnut oil," said my mother.

"I thought it was something because everything is always so shiny in here. And it always smells nice in here. Now you tell Buddy, when he pulls up the dandelions this year to save 'em for me, so I can make my wine."

"All right."

"I'll make some dandelion wine and I'll make some strawberry wine."

"I love strawberry wine."

"I'll bring you some."

"Have you ever had straw wine?"

"I don't think I'd like any wine made out of straw."

"They don't make it out of straw; they dry the grapes on straw. Then they make the wine. Maybe it gives it a straw taste."

"Now who would want wine with a straw taste?"

"Some people might. I know people like beer, which I don't like. Sam brought me some champagne when he came home from the Great War. I was amazed by the taste of that."

"Yes, it is good. But I'm a beer drinker from way back. . . . At first Mag wouldn't even let me touch her hair. She's superstitious about the hair and thought it would be crazy to let me touch her hair. It was Miss Leeds that persuaded her, and she trusts Miss Leeds above them all. I don't know anybody else she does trust, except Shawnee Man, you know, Sam's friend. She told Mag I was an itinerant beautician, using the same word as Sam, whatever that means. Sometimes I do use some of Miss Leeds's beauty products, because some of them are just as good or better than the store-bought variety and kind. And I use an antique basin that Miss Leeds says hairdressers and barbers used to use in the old-timey days. I carry that about with me. Sometimes I even wear it on my head like the old-time barbers used to do. It looks sort of like a helmet. I haven't got Mag her crowning glory back, but her hair doesn't break off so much. Mag trusts Miss Leeds."

"I think that's because you're a trained beautician, though, not just Doc Leeds's products. I think Mag's hair broke off because she started doing her own hair, not because of some hoodoo. But you can't tell Mag that."

"No, you can't tell Mag that."

"I see you've got some of Mag's doilies."

"I'm patient enough to do hair, even extravagant designs," said Delilah. "But I'm not patient enough to make doilies."

"Few people are."

"Sometimes I let Mag pay me in doilies instead of cash."

"That's called the barter system."

"I don't know what it's called, but that's what we do sometimes. And those doilies are worth more than cash. She's a real artist."

"I know she is."

When I get back to Gladys's, I pull half a bag of popcorn out of my pocket and start to chew.

"You always do that," she says. "I always gobble my popcorn in the movies and then when we get back here you pull out yours."

"Yeah," I say. I start to make a joke, but I don't.

"I like to eat it while it's still hot and buttery," she says. I make a joke. She tosses her big pillow and me.

"I thought you were a serious fellow when I first met you," she says. "But you also like to joke around."

I explain to her that ever since I was a youngster, a little boy, I liked to reserve my popcorn for outside the movies.

"I bet you went to shoot-'em-ups," she observed. "I bet you played cops and robbers and cowboys and Indians."

"As a matter of fact I didn't," I said. "I saw the movies, but my father wouldn't allow me to play the cops or the robbers, the cowboys or the Indians. And he also had an Indian friend named Mr. Dancing."

"Dancing Bear?" she asked.

"No, of course not. Nobody called him out of his name."

"You're still a jokester, though, Buddy Ray Guy."

"Aunt Maggie, how come nobody's found you yet?" I asked when I was a little boy.

"Who told you I was lost?"

I explained to her that I'd overheard my mother and Miss Delilah, the neighborhood lady that did her hair, talking about finding people, and that a man named Mr. Wayman had found Delilah or that she'd found him.

Aunt Maggie laughed and then she said, "When I get lost, I'll let the gentleman know."

She worked on one of her doilies. She seemed like she wanted to say something about Miss Delilah and finding men, but she didn't. Instead she hummed a little tune, which I recognized later as "Wild Women Don't Get the Blues." I played with a pair of Chinese handcuffs she'd brought back from the Kentucky State Fair.

I started to ask her if she'd ever been in love, because I knew that's what the women were talking about when they were talking about finding men, but I didn't dare ask. I just played with the Chinese handcuffs. I couldn't get them off, until Aunt Maggie told me their secret.

"Push in. Now pull," she said. "There, you've got it."

"Peel some extra potatoes, Buddy," said the sergeant in charge of the mess. "We've got some POWs now. Got to feed them too."

Codes of conduct in wartime. He started grumbling about the provisions.

All's fair in love, like war, they say. But all's not fair in love or war. Suppose I were to kidnap the Unicorn Woman, drag her off by the hair? There are codes of conduct in love and warfare. Rules to follow. Laws.

Sometimes Aunt Maggie would talk to me about love or, rather, I would ask her questions.

"Why do people say fall in love?"

"You mean, why not rise in love? That's a good question. I don't know the answer myself. I used to wonder about that expression myself when I was little."

Would I love the Unicorn Woman without her horn? Why do I say love?

Aunt Maggie muses. "Somebody once said the road to love is long and diffi-cult. I don't know who that somebody was. Maybe I just make the road to love longer and harder than it is. I used to think I was in love with Mr. Dancing. You know, your dad's buddy. I told you I danced with him once at Tiger's Inn. But that was more fascination, I guess, and admiration, and he was a different sort of man. Sometimes I'm attracted to different sorts of men. I guess I'm not alone in that. Why am I telling a little boy this? Why don't you ask your mama and daddy about love? Anyway, I told Mr. Dancing we all ought to be paying the Indian peoples for the use of their country. . . . He seemed surprised to hear that from me. . . . I think he has a darling somewhere out west. He goes out there every now and then to one of the reservations out there. But he prefers to

stay off the reservation. I don't think he was ever on any reservation himself.
But we all ought to pay for the use of the Indian lands."

"Isn't it our country too?" I asked. "Didn't we work long and hard for it too?"

"Like the road to love, eh? Sam is always telling you about the slavery days.
You're just a little boy."

"Daddy says I'm not too young to hear our story."

"Some of us were free people."

She mused again. Then she said, "I thought Mr. Dancing should love me
because I spent all my time thinking of him. I thought he should spend some
time thinking of me. Some people have true love and some people have deep
love, and there are many different kinds of love. But I think he has a darling
on one of the reservations out west in Arizona or New Mexico or someplace like
that that he goes to visit every now and then. I think he might have sons and
daughters, for all I know. I don't think he's your dad's buddy."

I used to think that whenever anybody said "buddy," they were calling my
name. Then I learned better.

I put the Chinese handcuffs back on, pushed in and took them off again.

"Now you understand," she said.

I didn't know whether she was talking about love, the different kinds of love,
or the Chinese handcuffs. Or even about Mr. Dancing and his darling on the
reservation in the Wild Wild West.

Once I asked her where Mr. Dancing came from.

"His people have always been around here. They never marched off to the
reservations, like I told you. They stayed around here. They were here for thou-
sands and thousands of years and so they stayed here."

Then she quoted to me what she called an African American proverb: "Tell
me whom you love and I'll tell you who you are."

She looked darker than the first time I saw her. When I first saw Doc Leeds
she looked as fair as a white woman. Almost like an Irish woman, like my
Aunt Maggie had told me she'd look. But perhaps that was her winter
face. Now she has darkened in the summer sunlight. She was the color of
light-brown toast, but no one would have mistaken her for white, even Irish,
though I've seen Italian women of her complexion and some women from

Southern France and Southern Spain. All kinds of Southern Europeans. I know for sure now it's not shadow.

I sat down in the other wicker chair and listened to *Amos 'n' Andy* with her. In the radio show, Andy is tricked by Kingfish again. Kingfish again gains something of Andy's, not money this time. I can't remember exactly what, but it's somehow more important than money. Still, when Kingfish gains it, he makes Andy feel as if he's doing the right, just, or moral thing by giving it to him. Then, of course, Amos arrives to explain the trick and Kingfish as the trickster:

"You ought not to listen to Kingfish," says Amos.

"The last time you told me to listen to him."

"I said to listen to him right, but you insist on listening to him wrong."

"I listened to every word he said and I thought I understood him."

"Well, maybe the problem, Andy, is you got to think about a thing more than once. You've got to think about a thing two or three times. Kingfish has a quick and agile mind, but he certainly misuses it on you. He's like the fox and you're like the baffled, bumbling bear. You've got to possess more wiliness around Kingfish."

"Well," says Andy, "I'll try to take your advice and think several times when I listen to Kingfish, but I guess Kingfish, with his quick, wilderness mind, has misused me again."

"Goodnight, Andy."

"Goodnight, Amos."

"Goodnight, folks in radio land."

Of course this is not a transcript of the exact program broadcast that day and only my reimagining of it. Kingfish was always the trickster in the story. Finally, Doc Leeds turned off the radio and said, "That Andy is something else, ain't he?"

"Yes ma'am, he sure is," I said.

"It'll take Andy to confuse wiliness and wilderness. But what bear wouldn't? I see you haven't brought your Unicorn Woman. Have you found her yet?"

"Not yet. I've got more clues to where she is, but I haven't found her yet. She's no longer with the carnival but with a troop called Wiley's Wonders."

"Speaking of wiliness," she laughed. "In the army?"

"No, it's like a circus troop or a carnival troop of exotic types and all sorts of oddities, but not a full carnival. I guess they troop around displaying the bizarre types, but it's not a full carnival show."

"That just tells you they can be anywhere, maybe even overseas."

"I think they just travel in this country, perhaps overseas as well, but I couldn't guess where. I haven't seen any posters advertising them."

She got up and went in the house and came back and handed me a brochure.

"This is what someone printed up for me," she said. "You can read it later. It's my advertisement. I never thought I needed to advertise. But this is the modern day and age."

I put it in my pocket.

"Well, I see your sympathy symptoms have cleared up right nicely."

"Yes, ma'am, thank you."

She stared out at her ducks and chickens, and rocked a bit in her wicker chair. One of the chickens tried to bust out of the yard, and she got up and chased it back, very agilely for an older woman. Then she came back and sat in the wicker chair. I leaned back in my wicker chair, saying nothing, appreciating the clear air and the sunshine and the green grass. The strong smell of the black walnut tree. I sat upright.

"Now what you have," she said, "is one of those maladies of the spirit. I can't cure that."

"Do you read the future?" I asked.

"Not a word of it. What do you want to know?"

"If I'll find her."

"I don't know. You'll either find her or you won't. But there's another possibility."

"What's that?"

"That she'll find *you*."

I sighed. "But she's not looking for me."

"You don't know that for sure, mister. You never know for sure who's looking for you. It surprises me all the time the people that come here to find me. And half of them don't even know they were looking for me. But now that I've got my advertisements, I can direct people. And I can give them to people that I want to find me."

She rocked in her wicker chair. I started to take out a cigarette but didn't want to smoke in front of her. I rose up when I saw others heading for the porch.

I drove to Railroad Street and parked. I thought of Aunt Maggie dancing in the street after the war had ended. I thought of Mr. Dancing, who didn't dance when the war was over but had danced with Aunt Maggie at Tiger's Inn. I thought of her discussions of being in love with him. I thought of the African American proverb about love. I had also come across an African proverb about love from Nigeria: "You know who you love, but you can't know who loves you."

I wondered whether Mr. Dancing truly had a darling on a reservation somewhere in the West who he went to visit every now and then.

I imagined myself dancing in the street with the Unicorn Woman, until the town deputy sheriff came up to my car and pounded on the window.

He asked me what I was doing there and said something about sleeping vagrants, and that they didn't allow vagrants in their town.

I straightened and leaned forward. I didn't know whether to start the ignition or wait for him to speak again. I knew the man, or rather knew about him, but I knew he didn't know me. I was cautious. I kept my hands on the steering wheel and tried not to make any sudden moves he might misinterpret. I tried to remember all the lessons I had learned when being stopped by patrol officers.

"You from these parts?" he asked.

"Lexington, sir. But I have people who live in this town." I told him where I worked. I didn't tell him what type of work I did; I just told him where.

He said if I wanted to sleep in my car, I'd better go where the people knew me. Then he waved me on, and I started the ignition.

On the highway, I pulled to the soft shoulder of the road, relaxed, and took out my cigarettes and the brochure that Doc Leeds had given me.

When I opened it, it said simply:

VINE EGERIA LEEDS, HERBOLOGIST

So it wasn't Vinnie Leeds but Vine E. Leeds. People were always calling her out of her name and didn't know it. Her name was printed on the brochure, and her address and a map showing how to get to her destination. There was also a recipe for yam and collard-greens stew and an advertisement for something she called a "complete food bar," which resembled a candy bar except its ingredients were fruits, vegetables, whole grains, nuts, pumpkin and sunflower seeds, greens, coconut, and peanut butter. They were referred to as "nutritionally complete food bars, for a nutritional, complete meal." She also sundried the fruits and vegetables: cauliflower, broccoli, cabbage, beans, yams, tomatoes, radishes, spinach, spring onions, collard greens, apples, blueberries, coconut, apricots, bananas, pineapples, grapes, green tea and whole milk . . . then she fashioned them into bars with various combinations of grains and rices and nut butters. She even used something she called "ancient grains."

I remembered seeing Aunt Maggie eating some kind of bar wrapped in wax paper and now figured it must be something she had obtained from Doc Leeds. I had asked her if I could have a piece of her candy bar and she had said no, that it was fashioned just for her and her constitution.

I smoked my cigarette, thought about "internal pollution" and pollution in general, then pulled back onto the highway and drove to where I thought the people knew me.

I was sitting in the Spider Web bar and restaurant drinking a beer when I saw Esta walk by. Remember Esta, the woman who should have been named Easter, my former sometimes girlfriend? I rushed to the door and called her. She was carrying an armload of books.

"Hey, Esta, how are you?"

I started to say "darling" but caught myself. She looked at me like I was the spider beckoning her into my web. Then I thought of an African spider my father had taught me about named Anansi. My father said he was a trickster and known among all the African peoples in their tales and stories and so I should know about him too. My father said he was the god of the knowledge of stories and storytelling. My father wasn't much for talking but sometimes he'd share bits of wisdom with me. So I tried to look like Anansi, the original Spider Man, the King of Stories.

"Some Africans in America think they're saying 'Aunt Nancy,'" my father explained. "They have tales of Aunt Nancy. But I'll tell you the true tales."

"I'm on my way to work," Esta explained. She looked at me like you'd look at a trickster. Or maybe she wasn't used to seeing me in the Spider Web.

"Well, you can spare a little time, can't you, girl? Come on in and have a drink with me." I'd never called her "girl" before, not even "my girl."

"I'll just have a Coca-Cola," she said, coming in and setting the book on the tabletop.

"I work at the Lexington Public Library now and clean up after hours," she explained.

I examined the books. They were translations from the French.

"You're not supposed to check books out of the library. That's against the law. Did you sneak these out?"

"No, Buddy Ray. The head librarian saw me looking through them and checked them out for me. I'm not supposed to tell anybody though. I put them in a laundry bag and leave them in a special place. You were doing all that French talk, so that got me interested in French writers and I was glancing at them when the librarian spotted me. Like Molière. I thought she was going to fire me for loafing, but she didn't. She checked them out for me. She behaved like a lot of our people would do. Of course, she told me to get back to work. Then she explained to me her stratagem. But she behaved like I was the first colored person to open a book."

"Well, it's good to see you're improving your mind."

She gave me an odd look. She said nothing. She took a laundry bag out of her purse and stuffed the books in.

"You're still in the neighborhood?" I asked.

"Yes, Buddy Ray. I'm not a gadabout like you. You are rather like a homing pigeon, though. They always find their way home. You're the one who told me how they used to deliver their messages during the war and about the Confidential Pigeon Service. I didn't know pigeons were that smart. But I'm seeing somebody. I don't want to play with you."

I ordered another beer and asked if she wanted another Coke. I didn't remember telling her about the use of homing pigeons in the war, but I must have.

"No thanks. I'd best be off to work. I don't abuse anybody's generosity."

She twisted the laundry bag and held it in her fist, then she slung it over her shoulder. Her purse dangled from her other hand.

"Are you still hunting unicorns?" she asked.

"Yes."

"Well, my unicorn found me, and he's a real nice man too, and he's not a sometimes person. He's not a gadabout like you. And I'm the one who gives him the incentive he needs and he also derives incentive from himself, not some unicorn woman. Are you going to have another beer?"

"No, this is my limit," I said.

"Well, that's good. I don't want you to be no drunkard."

I told her that I had learned that the French in the seventeenth century spoke very slowly, but as the rhythm of life speeded up, they began to speak faster, and that though the rhythm and vocabulary of their speech suggested contemporary times, the velocity of the speech did not. I suggested that that was probably why city people spoke faster than country people, and Northerners spoke faster than Southerners.

I watched her walk down the street with her laundry bag, then I ordered another beer.

I think of Gladys as I drive toward Memphis. Perhaps Gladys had told Wooley to give me her whereabouts, and Wooley had taken it upon herself not to. I can't believe that Gladys would have left without sending some word of where or how I could find her. After all, we'd been close friends.

But when I drive up to Wooley's, the boardinghouse itself is boarded up. I park and walk up onto the porch anyway. There's a for-sale sign tacked to one of the boards and underneath in small letters: terms negotiable. I know for sure this is one of the few boardinghouses where colored people stay. But there's no address indicating where or how one could buy this house. Perhaps interested buyers are only limited to those who already know Wooley and where she's residing now. And who have the sufficient capital to purchase a boardinghouse.

I lean against the railing and light up a Philip Morris cigarette.

After a while the door across the street opens and a man comes out waving and walking toward me. His biggish pants are dancing on their suspenders. He's shaped like a hurdy-gurdy but seems as agile as a black bear. It's the black bear and not the brown one that's the tree-climbing bear.

"Who you setching for?" he asks.

"Cousin of mine."

"Wooley?"

"Naw, one of her boarders."

"Wooley moved, ain't no boarders." He chuckles. "That I know about."

"Where did Wooley move to?"

"I know generally whereabouts, but not the particulars."

"Where generally?"

"She went up north, to Alaska."

"Alaska?" I repeat. I'm incredulous.

"Yes, sir. I told her she'd be disillusioned up in Alaska. I asked her why not Canada? But she said she wanted Alaska. I told her she'd freeze her butt off that far north. But she got it in her mind to move up there, to get as far north as she could get. When she gets up to Alaska, she won't have any more illusions about the North."

"I don't know," I say. I offer him a cigarette.

"No thanks. I don't smoke. A lot of colored folks come here looking for her boardinghouse. I don't know who's going to purchase it and whether they're going to keep it as a boardinghouse or renovate it. My name's Milton, by the way."

"How do you do? I'm Buddy."

"Oh, you're the one that travels the southern roads. I think I heard Wooley mention you. She expressed some concern about it. I never boarded with Wooley. But I used to go over there sometimes for her pancakes, and we'd have a chat. She makes the best pancakes in the world. Did you ever get a taste of those pancakes?"

"Yes."

"Best pancakes in the world. And a fine cup of coffee. And those hominy grits. I tried to court her once, but it didn't work out. I don't think she appreciated to be courted. Now she's up there in Alaska somewhere. Well, I hope Alaska appreciates who they got. I don't know what the Alaskan cuisine is like. And I don't know what the percentage of us colored people is in Alaska. She said she might go amongst the Athabaskan people, whoever they are, and if they'll welcome her."

He says so long and crosses the street. I stand and smoke another cigarette, then walk to the car.

"We had this Englishman preacher to come to our church," says Gladys.

"I never really thought of you as a churchgoer," I say.

She looks at me with amusement. "Yes, Buddy Ray, I do go to church. Aren't you religious?"

"About as religious as they come."

"Is that supposed to be dirty?" she asks.

"No."

"I can't tell when you're saying something dirty. One of those double entendres."

She sucks on a cigarette instead of puffing on it. She's fun to watch.

"Anyway, this Englishman preacher came all the way from England. He was visiting churches in the South and he wanted to visit a colored people's church. Our reverend introduced him, because we were wondering what that white man was doing sitting up in our church and behaving like he belonged there. You couldn't tell he was an Englishman until he started talking. Well, he did dress kind of oddly and had a certain air about him. We had supper for him, prepared by the ladies of the church, and I got to sit beside him at the table. I don't know why they picked me to sit beside him."

"Because you're very comely," I say.

"I know that's a double entendre."

"I sing in the choir, and perhaps he did notice me. Maybe he asked. I don't know. But someone said, 'Sister Wimbleton, you sit here,' so I sat down. I didn't want to sit beside him because I'm not the highest woman in the church and not an officer of the church. But our reverend nodded to me, so I sat down. The first thing he said to me was 'Can I assist you to some mashed potatoes?' That's what the Englishman said. People are not used to that kind of talk or to white people serving you instead of you serving them. So everybody was just a-looking and a-listening, you know. And he didn't just hand me the bowl of mashed potatoes; he spooned them onto my plate. Just like he was serving me. I wasn't used to that. And he said, 'I'm not unused to colored people.' And then he started talking about being a missionary in Africa and India and such places. Instead of saying he was used to colored people, he said he was not unused to them. I'm glad he wasn't a soldier who fought in those distant native lands and was a missionary. He talked about Africa and India and he talked about England and English porridge. And then he started telling me about fox hunting. He said that the fox was as thrilled by being hunted, I mean, that the fox experienced the thrill of the chase the same as the hunter and that the craftiness and the wiliness of the fox was actually developed because of fox-hunting stratagems and trying to outwit the hunter. I didn't really believe him, or like that kind of talk, but I listened and everybody at the table was listening and nobody challenged him. But I don't think that a fox enjoys being hunted. Then I thought about playing hide-and-seek when I was a little girl and I felt pleasure when I was hiding and pleasure when people found me, so maybe he was correct in his estimation of the fox. . . . Before we all sat down to dinner, a young girl read a poem that has been circulating amongst the colored churches and sounded like it had been especially prepared for the Englishman, because they like odes and poetry. Perhaps they even invented the ode.

IN GOD WE TRUST
In God we trust
For a sound mind,
At our awakening dawning,
That the day be gay,
With a cheerful morning,
That we greet each meal
With a humble thanks to God,
With peace and good will
And a happy heart
That all through the day
If we may perchance
Some poor soul we could lead,
Lifting our hearts to pray
Thankful that we've done our deed,

In God we trust,
That through the day
Our talents we have used
Our duty done, with great fulfilment
That no one we've abused
For when the shadows begin to creep
And we breathe a little prayer
In God we trust, while asleep
Our night watch, He will share.

"I still remember it, because everybody in the congregation had to learn it. I have a good memory for church matters. If they called women to preach, I would love to sermonize. And the Englishman seemed like he appreciated the ode as if it were written in his own language, I mean the way that English people speak."

"How was his sermon?" I ask. "Didn't he give a sermon?"

"Yes. We were all expecting one of those long sermons, because that's what we're used to, that's what our reverend gives, but he gave one of the shortest sermons I've ever heard."

"What did he say?"

"He said, 'I'm rather shy to come up here before you.' I've never heard of a shy preacher, but that's what he said. And the English don't seem like they are shy people. They seem like they are reserved people, but not shy. He said he didn't think of himself as an important man, but that he had an important duty. He said he was the least flycatcher for the Lord. I didn't know what he meant until the preacher explained to us that a flycatcher was a bird, and that the least flycatcher is the smallest of those birds. Because, you know, some of the church people were offended when he called himself a flycatcher, because some people call colored people flies in the buttermilk, you know. And then he said something about virtue being its own reward. That's all he said, and then he sat down and let our reverend talk, and all he did was listen." She pauses and then she says, "He's the first genuine Englishman I've ever met. The only English people I've met have been in books and in the movies. Of course I've heard them on the radio. In some of the romances I read, sometimes they have English men and women falling in love with somebody, or somebody falling in love with them. And, of course, like I said, I've seen them in the movies and heard them on the radio. I used to listen to them a lot before and during the war. News from the British home front and detective shows and of course Winston Churchill when he would want to inspire the people and some of the royals, when the king and queen would give their speeches and we read English writers in school. . . . But because his sermon was so short, the choir started singing from a book of spirituals that was also circulating amongst the colored churches. Can I sing one of them for you?"

"Please do."

"It's called 'I'll Go to Nineveh and Preach.'

Old Jonah, he lived in a whale
Not doing God's will, he did fail
And hiding from God, he thought he was smart,
And ended up riding a sail,
The winds blew
The ship almost overturned
For their lives, the folk were concerned,
And they all cast lots,
Leaving Jonah in a spot,
He was cast out into the sea,
In the belly of the whale, God let him be.
Old Jonah, he prayed night and day, God, from me this curse, take away, I'll
*   go on to Nineveh and preach, God if you I can reach*
My fault for that fatal day,
To the ship I did stray.
And God heard Old Jonah's cry,
Now Jonah, I'll not let you die, Come out, oh Jonah, come out
Come out of your hiding place
And do what I told you to do.
My strength please renew it, You will I will do it,
For you I did reach,
I'll go to Nineveh and preach.

"You have a lovely voice," I say.

"I know I do," says Gladys. "I sing in the choir. Our reverend said the Englishman said it was the perfect preaching song. It's one of the new spirituals, like I said, circulating amongst the colored people's churches, because someone who attended one of our conventions said the spirituals were not just conceived in the old days but for the new days too. The writer of the new spirituals said that 'one's love of God is one's love for humanity.' I was supposed to recite one of the circulating odes for the English reverend also, but our preacher decided he didn't want to take up too much of the good reverend's time. Can I recite it for you, since I learned it anyway?"

"Go ahead. I'm learning something new about you all the time."

"I know."

Then she recited a poem she called "Ode to Guidance":

It is not the end of the day,
For this is the dawning
Never more to forget the Sincerity of the hours,
That compose our day,
But to fulfil each moment
With Love from the heart
And to remember the burdens
We share together
May sometimes be shared with others
It is not the end of the day
For this is the dawning
Bringing us hope and
Finding strength in it
To surpass our intrigued functions
To perform our duties
To know we are not
But together as one
It is not the end of the day
For this is the dawning
Teaching us the inevitable

Showing mercy bestowed upon us
Showing us the wealth of the earth
That we may perchance to inherit,
Notwithstanding our loneliness of heart
Easing our tensions
Helping us capture the meaning of life
Excusing the evil and
Accepting the good.
For at the end of the day
We may find the source
The secret of our being
The help for our souls
The advantages given us
All in all, as being immortal
Shallow yes, but not defeated
In event will be shown,
That we have the Holy Spirit
Within us
And God as our guide.

"That's the ode that was penned by the young woman at the Baptist convention that started her works circulating among the colored people and their churches. Well, I'm not sure whether she's a young woman or an old woman, and I'm not sure what 'intrigued functions' means. Do you like it? It's an ode, because, like I said, the English people are supposed to like odes, and this woman is a writer of odes as well as spirituals."

"Yes, it's quite nice."

"Now you're trying to sound like that English fellow. There is a revivalist church that publishes the spiritual and holy and religious writings of colored people, spirituals and sermons and poetry and odes and such, and circulates them among the various colored people's churches throughout, and amongst the saints and sinners."

"I believe I've come upon that church," I say. "I've seen and heard and read some of their literature, but I didn't know the writings were being circulated far and abroad."

"I can't picture you at any revival. I can picture you in warfare but not at any revival. I can't picture you reading religious literature either."

"I wasn't exactly at the revival, but I met the preacher. I was standing outside of his church and . . ."

"Yes, I can picture you standing outside of a church. My father fought in the first war. . . ."

"So did mine."

"That's something we have in common. He said they often made them take off their soldiers' uniforms, because it disturbed a lot of the white people to see colored men in uniforms."

"We're fighting the same war. My father used to speak that way and tell those sorts of stories. Just before I went off to war he wanted me to learn some things about the segregated and Jim Crow army. But he said our kin fought once in Revolutionary times. Men of our own family."

"And before Revolutionary times, but we've had preachers from different parts of the world come to our church. When they want to congregate with colored people, our preacher says, they come to the churches. Sometimes they invite themselves; sometimes we invite them. We had a preacher from Mexico and we had to learn one of the spirituals to sing to him in Spanish. There is a Mexican who is a member of our congregation who helped to invite him and taught us one of our spirituals in the Spanish version. The Mexican man sang the Spanish version and taught it to our choir and congregation; I hope I remember it correctly."

Necesito bendiciones
¡Oh! Señor, necesito bendiciones
Otorgado a mí,
Necesito bendiciones
¡Oh! Señor, necesito bendiciones
Otorgado a mí
Oh Señor, escucha mi llanto
Oh Señor, escucha mi súplica
Oh, precioso Jesús, por favor, respóndeme,
¡Oh Señor! Necesito bendiciones
Oh Padre celestial, que me has otorgado

Bendiciones para mis hijos—Oh Señor,
Bendiciones para mi pueblo—Oh Señor,
Bendiciones para mi nación—Oh Señor,
Bendiciones para mi país—Oh sí
Necesito estas bendiciones, oh Señor
¡Oh Señor! Escuchame,
Necesito bendiciones
Oh Padre celestial, que me has otorgado

"The visiting Mexican preacher preached in a combination of English and Spanish. But they are always having guest preachers at our church, like I said. Sometimes women will testify, but they do not preach. Once they called on me to testify, but I didn't know what to say."

"You don't seem like you have a loss for words."

"That's because I'm talking to you. That's not the same as talking to a congregation."

In a cabaret in Paris, right before I returned stateside, I met a woman whose name you wouldn't recognize. It wasn't Bricktop or Josephine Baker, or any well-known person, but she said she'd come to Paris before the war, or rather between wars, and had opened her own cabaret where she also performed. It wasn't just the fact that she'd traveled to Paris to open a nightclub and become a performer. She had pictures of herself hanging on her walls beside famous people you'd recognize, famous writers and actors and entertainers. Sometimes politicians. Everybody who had a word or two with the famous liked to have their pictures taken with them, and she was no exception. Plus, she said, it was good for business. She sang in a straight and simple way and played a cornet as she sang. The singing was straight and simple but the music wasn't. Notes and melodies swerved, collided, diverged, circled, and hovered, flew backwards, sideways, up and down and forward. It reminded me of a hummingbird. Or some sort of craft in a futuristic story. I liked her voice, but I preferred to hear her play the cornet, which I wasn't used to women doing.

She had a long mirror covering the whole back wall of the cabaret, and when she sang or played the cornet she didn't turn directly to face her audience the way most every performer does; she'd turn toward the mirror and look at her audience through the mirror. They looked at her through the mirror and she looked at them through it. I'm not sure if it was shyness or a strategy.

She had tales of all the famous people who'd come to Paris before and after the war and ordinary folks too. Names known and unknown.

Ernest and James and Scott and Gertrude and Paulette and Humphrey and Cab and Albert and Edgar and Charlie and Orson and Otto and Ethel. She said all their names like everyday names. She said their names like she knew them personally.

One day I notice that the tractors that Grange and I have been working on have suddenly gotten cleaner. I don't mention this to Grange. I can't figure it out. Then I notice that one especially dirty tractor had been especially dirty one day and the next day is especially clean. It even looks as if someone has polished it. I still don't mention this to Grange, and he doesn't seem to notice.

The next night in the middle of the night, I get dressed and drive out to the workplace. Sure enough, she's up on one of the tractors with a scrub brush and a chamois rag, scrubbing and polishing feverishly. I park a bit up the road but where I can still see her. I light a cigarette and watch. She pushes her hair back from her forehead and scrubs like the whole world depends upon it. Remember Kate? The woman Grange said had the tractor repair job during the war, when women did the work of men on the home front and for the war effort, and then when the war was over and the men returned, she got fired? The boss had offered her a job polishing the tractors, but she wouldn't take it. But now she's doing exactly that. I don't know if she's getting paid for cleaning and polishing the tractors or whether it's something she's just doing. Whether it's some personal obsession and compulsion. I watch her for a good fifteen minutes. If Grange notices anything about the clean and polished tractors he doesn't say anything. I don't give away her secret. I keep waiting for her to bust a few tractors or sabotage us, but she doesn't. She just cleans and polishes them.

———————

I ride around the colored neighborhood until I see a sign that says "Rooms for Rent."

"Where's your bag?" the woman at the door asks.

"It's in my trunk."

"Go get it and bring it with you. I don't allow men to come in here that don't have bags. It don't look decent. This is a respectable place."

I go and get my bag out of the trunk and a pamphlet out of my glove compartment and come back to the porch.

"What did you pull out of your glove compartment?" she asks, looking wary. "What's that piece of paper you got?"

I show her the advertisement for Wiley's Wonders.

"On vacation, are you? Going to the carnival?"

"Yes, ma'am," I say.

Upstairs, I sleep. I dream of Grande Otelo, the little black Brazilian I'd seen in the movies when I was a boy. He's part of Wiley's Wonders, along with the Unicorn Woman.

Você às vezes não sente que há uma tempestade dentro de você?
Sim.
Você já teve sonhos que o guiam?
Sim.
Você entende a arquitetura de um sonho?

In this dream, I speak Portuguese fluently or so it seems to me, then I enter another dream.

In this new dream, I'm sitting on a stool in an empty tent. I'm roped off. Then people enter, wearing masks, individuals and whole families.

They mill about, observing me and whispering, then they begin talking loud enough for me to hear.

"I don't see why Wiley put him in here with his wonders. What makes him a wonder? He looks like an ordinary colored man to me. Just an ordinary fellow. There's nothing odd about him except for his wild hair."

"Look, Skeeter; he looks like that gingerbread man you baked this morning."

"Left it in the oven too long."

———————

When I wake, I go downstairs to breakfast. I discover that Mrs. Pergamon, who's the owner of the boardinghouse, runs her kitchen much like Wooley Boatman, except her cooking is not as good. It's respectable, but it's nothing to rave about. I'm sitting at the kitchen table, alone, eating cold pancakes when she comes in.

"Let me heat those for you, mister," she says.

"No thank you, ma'am; this is fine."

"I heard somebody in here and didn't know who the straggler was, because everybody else has breakfast right early. We're all early birds around here. You're the only one who's on vacation. We other folks have to get up early and go to work or go looking for work. Where you from?"

"Lexington, Kentucky, ma'am."

"I know Lexington right well. I've been there several times. You look like a schoolteacher. Are you a schoolteacher?"

"No, ma'am."

"Those look like the eyeglasses of a schoolteacher. Or someone who spends their time reading books. But you've got the hands of a hardworking man. I've got some salve for your fingertips. I know they've got several colored schools there in Lexington."

"Yes, ma'am. Booker T. Washington, Frederick Douglass, Paul Laurence Dunbar, and George Washington Carver."

"Yes, I thought so. Y'all should have you a Harriet Tubman and a Sojourner Truth."

"Yes, ma'am."

"Well, I mistook you for a schoolteacher. Maybe it's the eyeglasses, like I said."

"Yes, ma'am."

"I've got 20/20 vision myself. What sort of working man are you?"

"I repair tractors."

"You don't say? I've ridden a few tractors in my day. I grew up on a farm, don't you know. But I dreamed of coming to the big city. So here I am."

I say nothing. I nibble my pancakes.

"Are you sure I can't heat those pancakes for you?"

"No thank you, ma'am."

"Can I help you to another cup of coffee?"

"Thank you."

She gets the pot from the stove and pours me another cup. I will say that her coffee is good. I tell her so.

"I don't see why," she says. "I take more time and care with my pancakes and other food offerings than I do my coffee, and everybody tells me my coffee is good, and nobody has anything good to say about my pancakes or other cuisine. Of course, you can't tell if the pancakes are good or not because you're eating them while they're cold. . . . What're those books you're reading? I knew you were a reading man."

She's just noticing the books I've got on the table.

"One's called *Southern Road* by Sterling Brown and the other's a book of poetry published and circulated by a revivalist church."

"Colored authors?"

"Yes, ma'am."

"That one there don't look colored. Is that his picture?"

"Yes, ma'am. Sometimes he's been mistaken for a white man."

"Yes, I can imagine. Well, you do have schoolteacher ways," she says.

"I suppose so."

"Do you come to Memphis often?" she asks.

"Now and then. I used to stay at another boardinghouse, but they went out of business."

"Well, I hope you'll consider this your home," she says. "Especially if you are traveling these southern roads."

"I haven't been further south than Tennessee."

"Don't. I wouldn't recommend it, and you traveling all by your lonesome. And especially if these places are unfamiliar to you. You heard about the stranger in the strange land?"

"Yes, ma'am."

"I don't want you to be nobody's easy kill. You're a stranger, even if you know the territory. My preacher is always talking about the stranger in the strange land. That's about all he preaches about. And that's who you resemble. But some travelers and migrants from the deeper South, the deepest South, stop here on their way to the Deep North and do they have stories to tell. I don't want to spoil their illusion. I want them to stay with good people, leastwise while they're here. I thought I'd heard all the stories around here in Memphis. It's almost like this is a stage of the Underground Railroad that you hear stories about, except it's in modern times. So I wouldn't travel any further south all by my lonesome if I was you. Or up north either. That's why I call it the Deep North. I've been a wanderer myself. Don't you have any people?"

"Yes, ma'am."

"Well, I'm your people too. You can stay here whenever you're in town. People used to stay over at Boatman's—I think that's who you're talking about—but she sold out and left town and headed north. The North ain't all it pretends to be, like I said, though some people still consider it to be the promised land."

I get in my car and head north. Not too far north, just enough north to get out of Tennessee and back to Kentucky. While I'm repairing this new tractor, Grange starts talking about Daniel Boone, probably something he learned from his schoolteacher sister-in-law.

"You know, this is a historical place filled with historical people and historical towns. Daniel Boone was a smart man. You don't really think of Daniel Boone as smart, not book smart. You think of him as having common sense and natural sense, and being smart about the wilderness. But Daniel Boone had as much education as Daniel Webster, only he insisted on spelling a word the way it sounded. He knew how a word was supposed to be spelled, but he just insisted on spelling it like it sounded. If he shot a bar, he shot a bar."

I'm sitting in a bar drinking a beer and reading a couple of poems from the revivalist church publications.

"Hi, Buddy," she says, coming up to my table. It's Esta. "I thought you might be in here again. Somebody told me that you started coming here all the time after work and having a beer. I see you're reading. Can I sit down?"

"Sure," I say.

"I worry about you, Buddy," she says. "I hope you don't turn into a drunk. But I guess you'll be a literate drunk."

I say nothing.

"Would you like a Coke?" I ask.

"Yes, but I'll pay for it myself," she says, as I call the waiter over. She reaches in her laundry bag and takes out several books.

"The head librarian is still checking out books for me. She's a nice lady. I don't like her to break the law for me."

"Some laws are meant to be broken."

"That sounds like you, Buddy Ray. You're wilder and more complicated than you seem. But I don't want her to lose her librarian's license or anything like that. She seems like a good person and I don't want her to break the law for me. I don't want it to cost her her livelihood. She's an unmarried lady but she had an adventuresome life as a young woman. She was in Spain before the civil war and she's traveled to Mexico and been to different places before she settled down and became a librarian. I know that Mexicans are a brown-skinned people, so maybe that's why she is so enlightened for a person of this town, and of her age, but she was born and bred here. She talks to me like I'm a natural person. Some of the people don't accept you for a human being, but those are not her ways. Maybe it's because of her travels."

"Perhaps. Or perhaps it's just her nature."

"It could be her natural self. She doesn't tell me all of her business but I've learned some of it. I think she writes on the sly. I think she does some writing herself and is not only a librarian, but she hasn't shown me anything she's written. I think she writes short stories. She's a tallish woman and seems to have a real command of herself. She's of Irish ancestry. Her people fled Ireland and came to America. I don't know her whole story and I don't know what the library authorities would do if they knew she was providing me with books on the sly. She even got me a copy of some short stories by Langston Hughes and other forbidden classics that I know must be against the law."

I say nothing. I drink my beer and she sips her Coke.

"I can't afford to buy books the way that you do, Buddy Ray."

"I bought this one, and this one was given to me by a church that publishes the works of members of its congregation and colored people in the community. But he has global ambitions."

"What's the name of the church book?"

"*I Need Blessings: Poems, Song Lyrics, Spirituals, Prayers and Meditations.*"

"Are you a churchgoer now?"

"Not exactly. But I happen to know the preacher and sometimes I help him distribute his publications during my travels."

"That sounds like something you would do. Use your gadabout ways for some purpose. I go to the same church as your Aunt Maggie, so I know you don't attend our church."

I sip my beer.

"Do you want me to send you some books?" I ask her.

"No, Buddy Ray. Don't distribute your books to me. Anyway, you can't tell the saints from the sinners." She muses, then she says, "Are you still hunting for that Unicorn Woman or have you found her?"

"I'm still hunting."

"That sounds like you too. Gadabout."

She shrugs. She finishes her Coke and rises.

"See you, Buddy Ray." She stuffs her books into the laundry bag. I notice one of them is *Dubliners* by James Joyce, the "writer's writer," and several books of poetry by Federico García Lorca, *Book of Poems*, *Poem of the Deep Song*, and *Gypsy Ballads*. She also has a book of Yeats's poetry and an anthology of Irish literature. She puts a quarter on the table and scurries out.

I tear down the boards, rush in Wooley Boatman's and upstairs to Gladys's room. Inside, not Gladys, but the Unicorn Woman sits on the bed reading one of Gladys's romances.

"At last!" I exclaim, going to her. "At last I've found you. But what're you doing here?" I sit down beside her.

"I ran away from Wiley's Wonders, made my escape, and I'm hiding out here. It was just like slavery time. I thought you were the authorities, the patterrollers, coming to get me. He's alerted the authorities, the patterrollers, you know, and there are even advertisements for this runaway in the newspapers. I'm sure you've seen them in your day and age, patrolling for us."

"Let me take care of you. You need someone to take care of you."

"I worry about you too, Buddy Ray. Let's take care of each other." We embrace.

"Be careful," she says, as I come too near her horn. "You'll be a fugitive with me if you stay."

*I go downstairs, board up Wooley Boatman's, go around back, and climb in
through a window. I open Gladys's door. The Unicorn Woman is still sitting there.*

*"I've boarded us back up to steer the authorities away. But I don't know how
much freedom we'll have inside this place."*

*"I've got more freedom here than with Wiley's Wonders. He had me in a cage.
He didn't treat me like I was a human being. I've got a horn, but I'm still human.
But here I'm with you and I feel a sense of freedom. But I worry about you."*

"Me?"

"You seemed to have all the freedom in the world."

"Seeming ain't is," I say.

"But you seem as free as freedom."

"Seeming ain't is," I repeat.

*"Well, we've got each other," she says, smiling. "Come over here, Buddy
Ray, my love."*

Walking down Upper Street or up Upper Street one day, I see a sign:
REVIVALIST SERMON ABOUT UNICORN WOMEN AND OTHER ODDITIES.
I enter straightaway. It's the same preacher, the one I've been distributing
books for, unbeknownst to him, but he's older. There's gray peppering his
hair around his temples. I guess I can say the same about myself.

". . . I heard music in her tent. It wasn't church music, not spirituals. Like
I was telling you before, sometimes when the Lord wants to get your soul's
attention, he will manifest something in the physical. He manifested a horn
on this woman's head. She's not the only unicorn woman, but she's the only
such oddity that I've personally seen for myself. Sometimes the Lord directs
our footsteps to places of amusement like that when he wants us to bear
witness to a manifestation. The horn represents the soul's disequilibrium.
As soon as the woman gets her soul in equilibrium, the horn will disappear.
I saw a collection and selection of odd people parading themselves before
me. I observed them, so I can help to save y'all. . . . "

I can't bring myself to listen to the rest of the sermon, so I start to exit.
At the back of the hall, there are more publications by the revivalist church,
books, pamphlets, and broadsides. I gather a few and go outside. I sit on the
church steps, but I can still hear bits of the sermon, which sounds like poetry:

You might not see your horn,
But it's as real as the cornflakes you had this morning,
Real as the corned beef you had last night
Real as the cornerstone of this building
Real as Corn Chandler sitting over there nodding. Wake up, Brother Chandler,
I know you hear me
Real as the acorns on that tree outside
Real as the popcorn you chew on at the Lyric Theatre
Real as corn on the cob,
Real as a cornet,
Real as the cornet you play at Tiger's Inn
You hear me talking to you
Real as cornflowers in that field out there
Real as corn-poppy
Real as that corn starch you put on your face
All y'all got horns,
But they're invisible
Come up
Come on up
Come up
Yes I'm talking to you

I sit on the porch steps, reading a couple of the broadsides:

GOD DIDN'T SAY TO THE BLACK MAN HE MADE
God didn't say to the black man He made I'm making you black
As an ace of spade
For folks to trample and turn underfoot,
But I am making you
To start a new root,
God didn't say to the black man He made I am making you black to
   become a slave
But in the world you a place I do prepare
For you to raise your seed
And give them care

I'm making you free
As a sparrow in the breeze,
Or a robin that rests in the trees I'm making you with this black face
To become to me a special race
God didn't say to the black man He made,
The blackest of black
As the greenest of jade,
To be spat upon and scorned,
For you in your beauty
Are adorned
Are black
May have a pure soul
That the others lack.

When the preacher gets outside, he approaches me. "Don't I know you?" he asks.

"I came to one of your revivals some years ago," I say.

"I see you grabbed our publications, but you didn't stay inside," he says.

He gives me a good look. "I thought there was an air of familiarity about you. But you were a younger man and it was after the war. You didn't stay then, either, did you?"

"No, sir."

"What church are you a member of?"

"My folks belong to the Holy Pilgrim's Baptist Church."

"That's your folks; that's not you. Have you been baptized?"

"Yes, when I was a boy."

"And what brought you here today?"

"The sermon about the horn. I mean, the Unicorn Woman. I saw her years ago in Memphis."

"That's where she's still to be seen. I just came from a revival in Memphis and took a detour, and that's what led me to perceive the horn. She's a lovely woman. An older woman, but you can tell she was beauteous as a young one, and you can tell what she's been through. You can tell she's had struggles. I gave her a brochure and invited her to my revival. Needless to say, she didn't accept the invitation. But that horn has gotten hold of my imagination, and I use it in my sermons. I've seen photographs of drawings of other unicorn women, many different nationalities and many different ages and historical times. It's held onto my imagination. . . . When you get through reading our publications, circulate them among the people."

"I'll do that, sir. Yes, sir."

I don't tell him I'm already part of his troop of distributors.

"Some of them date back in time and others are from the modern day and time. The struggle continues."

"Yes, I know, sir. Do you mean the struggle in the spirit or the struggle in the world?"

He looks at me as if that was a foolish question, then he goes back into the church.

I drive to Wooley Boatman's at night, undo the boards, hurry up the stairs, lighting the way with my flashlight, open the door to Gladys's room. Of course, she's not there, nor is the Unicorn Woman, as I'd fancied in my dream. The room is empty, except for some scattered, abandoned romances on the floor. I gather them together, wipe the dust off of them on my sleeve, and carry them downstairs. I drive to the other boardinghouse, Mrs. Pergamon's, but it's too late to knock on Mrs. Pergamon's door, so I sleep in my car in the driveway. When I awake it's still too early to knock on Mrs. Pergamon's door, so I drive back to Kentucky.

When I get to my room, I open one of the romances. Gladys has scribbled in the margins: this is not love, not love, I don't believe this is love, not love at all, affection, desire, tenderness, fondness, then the question, "If people can think they're in love, can't they also think they're not?"

I was intrigued by the marginal notes, but not enough to read the romances. And not enough to search for Gladys.

"You kinda slowed up on your tractor fixing, ain't you, Buddy?" asks Grange. "You must be in love. I remember when I first met my wife, I mean before she became my wife, I kinda slowed down on my tractor fixing and became dreamy. When I asked her to marry me, I knew she'd say yes. Do you know how I knew?"

"How?"

"Because she'd slowed down too." I say nothing.

"You know what my wife was doing?"

"What?"

"Well, the same thing that I was doing."

"What's that?"

"Growing up."

Grange works on his tractor. I work on mine.

"They've started to hire some women to work out there at the tractor factory," says Grange. *"They experimented with them during the war, they needed them during the war, they got rid of 'em after the men came back, and now they've started hiring them again. They've hired Kate. I'm glad for that. Something to keep Kate busy."*

When I get off work, I drive to my parents' restaurant and sit drinking a beer. My parents are both elderly, but they still keep at work and still work together. My mother's polishing glasses, and my father's behind the counter prepping for the dinner people.

"Have you been back to Memphis?" my father asks.

"Yes."

My father goes back to prepping. I still haven't told them about the Unicorn Woman or those fanciful years. I suppose they think I just like Memphis.

"What'll you have?" my mother asks.

My father looks up. They're both golden in the sunlight, smiling at me, and waiting for my answer.